MUTTS
GO
GREEN

Other Books by Patrick McDonnell

Mutts
Cats and Dogs: Mutts II
More Shtuff: Mutts III
Yesh!: Mutts IV
Our Mutts: Five
A Little Look-See: Mutts VI
What Now: Mutts VII
I Want to Be the Kitty: Mutts VIII
Dog-Eared: Mutts IX
Who Let the Cat Out: Mutts X
Everyday Mutts
Animal Friendly
Call of the Wild
Stop and Smell the Roses
Earl & Mooch
Our Little Kat King
BONK!
Cat Crazy
Living the Dream
Playtime
Year of Yesh
#LoveMutts
You've Got Those Wild Eyes Again, Mooch
Hot Dogs, Hot Cats
The Mutts Diaries
The Mutts Winter Diaries
The Mutts Autumn Diaries
The Mutts Spring Diaries
The Mutts Summer Diaries

Mutts Sundays
Sunday Mornings
Sunday Afternoons
Sunday Evenings

Shelter Stories
A Shtinky Little Christmas

MUTTS

go GREEN

PATRICK McDONNELL

Andrews McMeel
PUBLISHING®

It is only a little planet,
but how beautiful it is.

- Robinson Jeffers

Keep it KIND, Keep it CLEAN, Keep it WILD, Keep it GREEN.

This planet is our home, a home we share with all people and all animals. A home that should be beautiful, safe, and happy for everyone. With earth under us, stars above, and plants and animals all around, we have much to appreciate.

The *Mutts* characters Earl, Mooch, and their furry friends try their best every day to make wise choices for themselves and for the earth—to keep it kind, clean, wild, and green. We can all do our part to make this world an even better place. I know you can do it. You are a force of nature! As Greta Thunberg says, and Shtinky Puddin' believes, you are never too small to make a difference.

Get inspired and do something. Some of the ideas in this book you can do on your own, while others may require help or permission from an adult.

Join the *Mutts* team in celebrating Earth Day every day.

—PATRICK McDONNELL

GO
GREEN

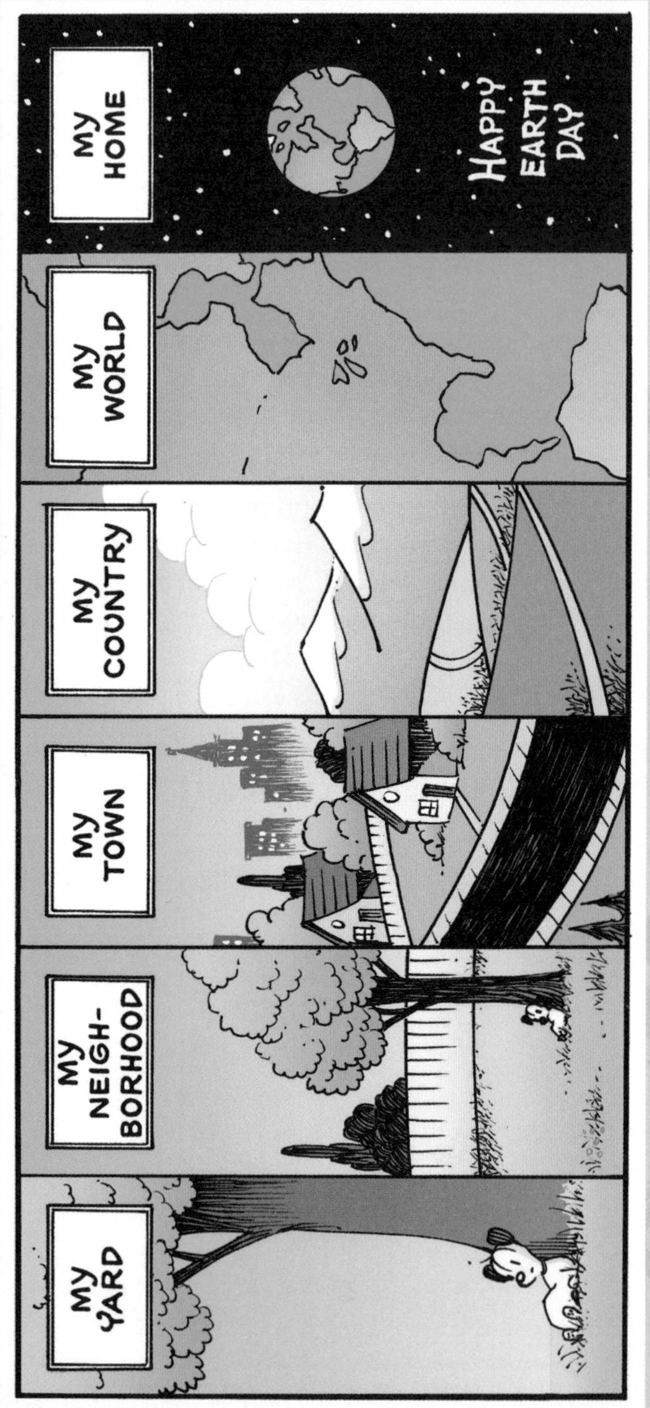

MY YARD
MY NEIGH-BORHOOD
MY TOWN
MY COUNTRY
MY WORLD
MY HOME
HAPPY EARTH DAY

THERE'S NO PLACE LIKE HOME.
SIGH...

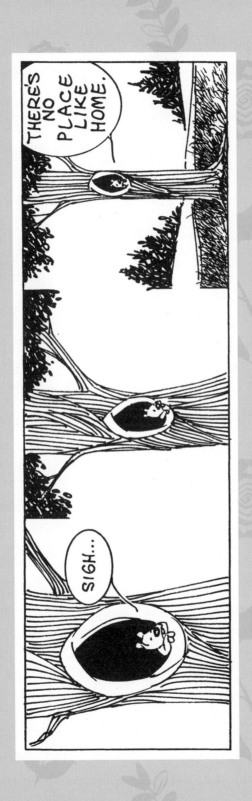

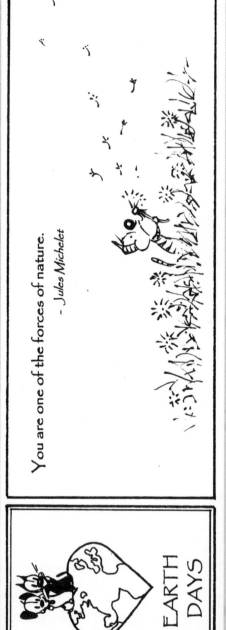

You are one of the forces of nature.

– *Jules Michelet*

EARTH DAYS

SHTINKY'S
TO·DO LIST
1. SAVE THE WORLD.
WOW
IT'S A GOOD THING I GOT UP EARLY.

Keep It KIND

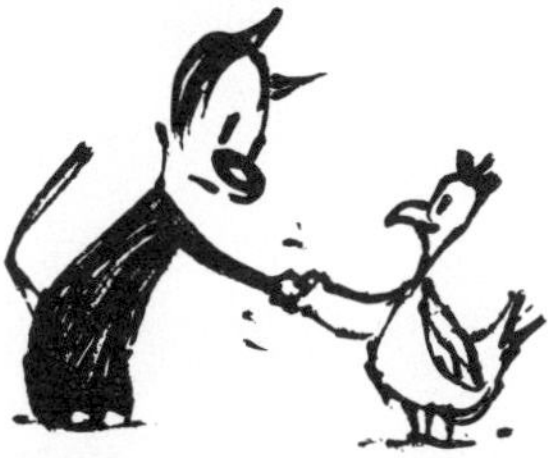

Kindness is at the heart of everything you can do to help the planet.

True happiness comes from making others happy. Thinking about other people and animals, and finding ways to make their lives better, can lift your spirits too. All animals have feelings, and all beings want to love and be loved.

An easy way to be kind is to adopt your own pets and to encourage your friends to find their new fur family members at local animal shelters. There are so many healthy, well-trained pets of all kinds just waiting for a family to love them. When you adopt, you save a life.

Making kind choices in what you eat and wear can also make a huge difference for everyone on this planet.

Together, we are one big family sharing this planet. When you practice kindness, the world changes for the better. It's simply in the way you look at things. When we have respect for all life, including bees, trees, flowers, animals, fish, and birds, to name just a few, we become more curious about the lives around us and more determined to help.

Three things in human life are important: the first is to be kind; the second is to be kind; and the third is to be kind.

—Henry James

How to Keep It Kind

◉ Be a helper.

◉ Practice empathy by imagining yourself in others' shoes.

◉ Adopt, don't shop. When you are ready to get your next pet, go to the animal shelter. Then, encourage your friends to do the same.

◉ Foster a homeless pet. Encourage your family to take in a dog or cat for a few weeks until they get adopted permanently.

◉ Volunteer for animal shelters by donating blankets or food. Make signs to decorate the shelter.

◉ When you celebrate your birthday, ask for donations, instead of gifts, to help animals or the environment.

◉ Make kind food choices, and go meatless at least one day a week.

◉ Go vegetarian or go vegan.

◉ Donate to a food pantry.

◉ Speak up for what you believe in and be nice at the same time.

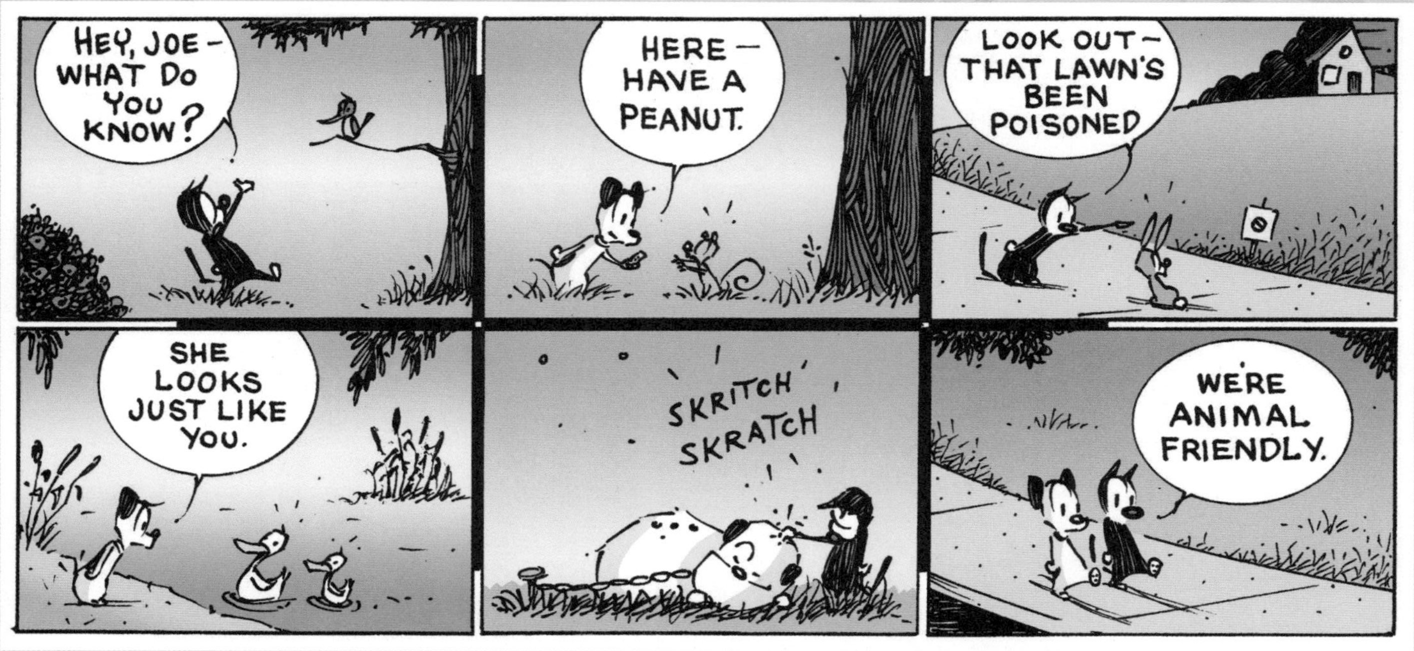
HEY, JOE - WHAT DO YOU KNOW?
HERE - HAVE A PEANUT.
LOOK OUT - THAT LAWN'S BEEN POISONED
SHE LOOKS JUST LIKE YOU.
SKRITCH SKRATCH
WE'RE ANIMAL FRIENDLY.

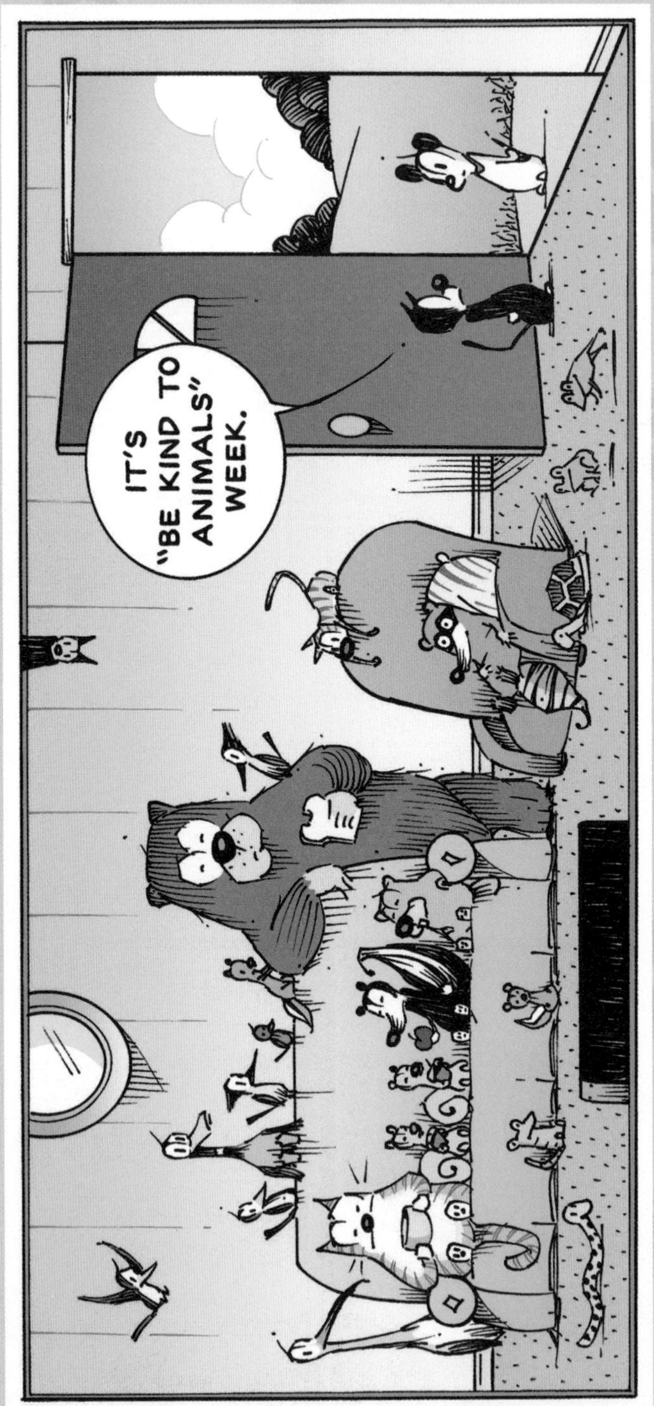
IT'S "BE KIND TO ANIMALS" WEEK.

BE KIND TO ANIMALS WEEK
BELLY RUB

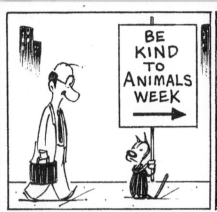

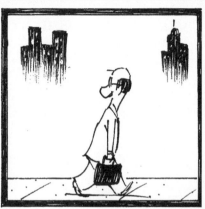

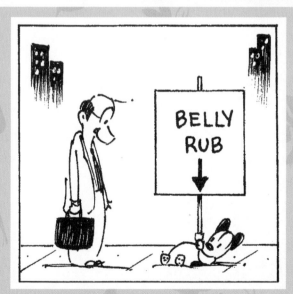

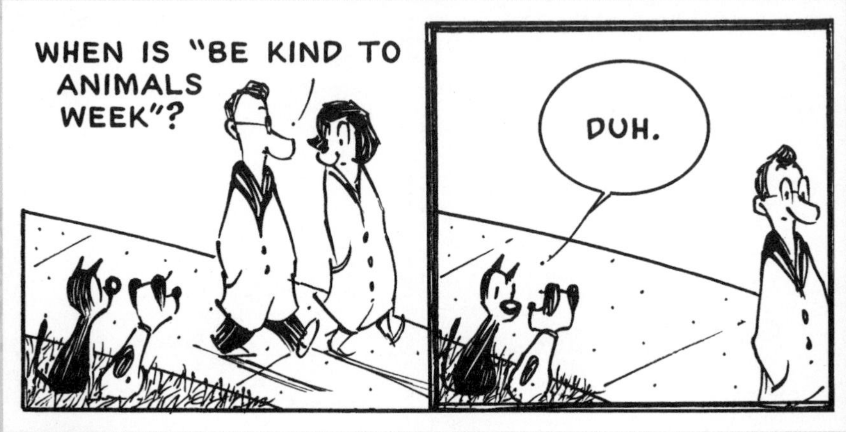
WHEN IS "BE KIND TO ANIMALS WEEK"?
DUH.

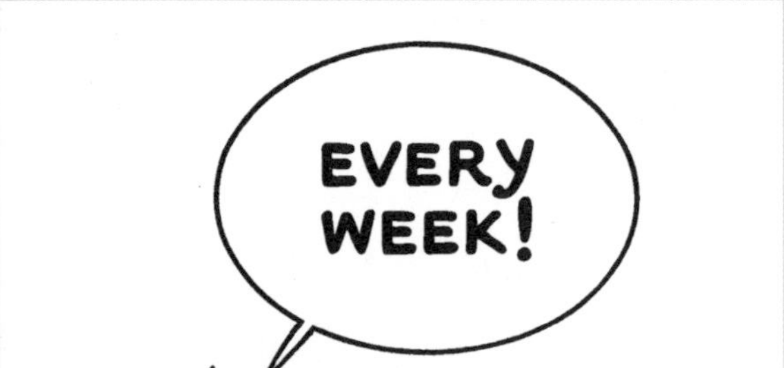
EVERY WEEK!

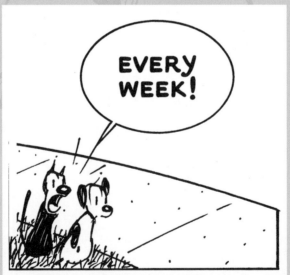

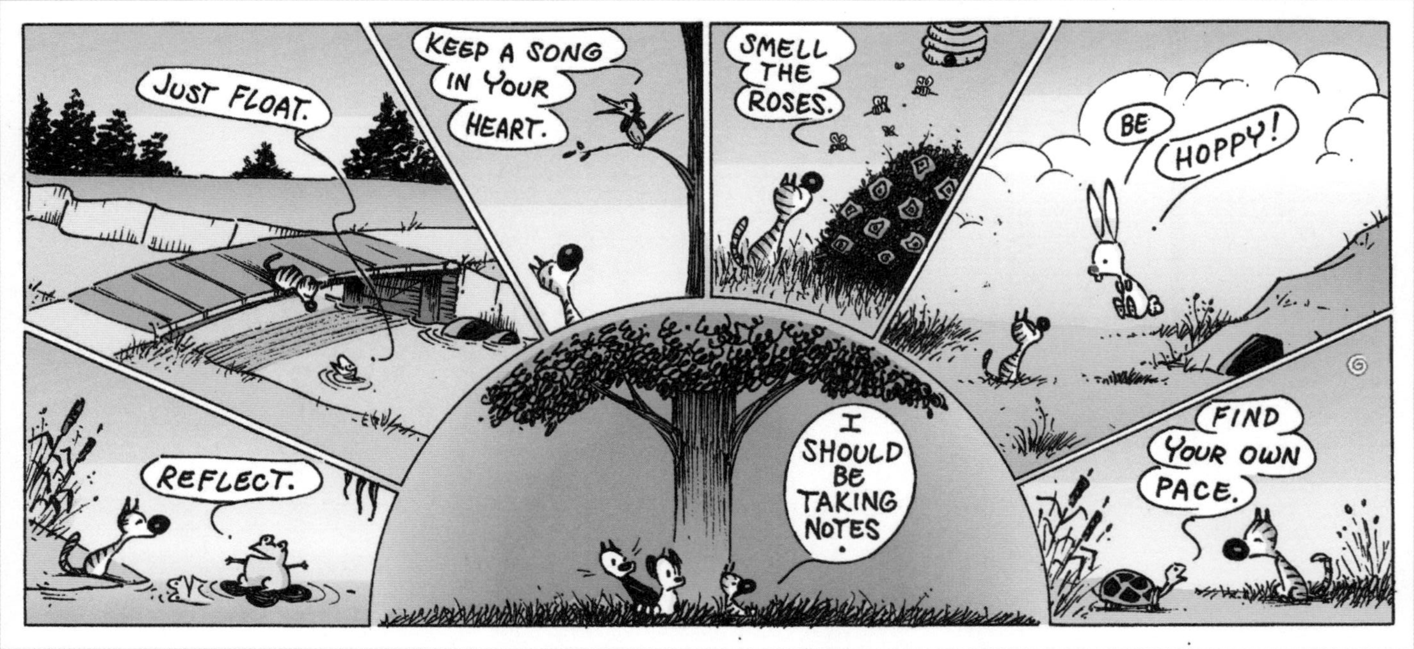
JUST FLOAT.
KEEP A SONG IN YOUR HEART.
SMELL THE ROSES.
BE
HOPPY!
REFLECT.
FIND YOUR OWN PACE.
I SHOULD BE TAKING NOTES.

WHAT'S ON THE LIST TODAY?
HMMM...
LIVE IN THE MOMENT AND LOVE ONE ANOTHER

THAT SHOULD KEEP US BUSY.

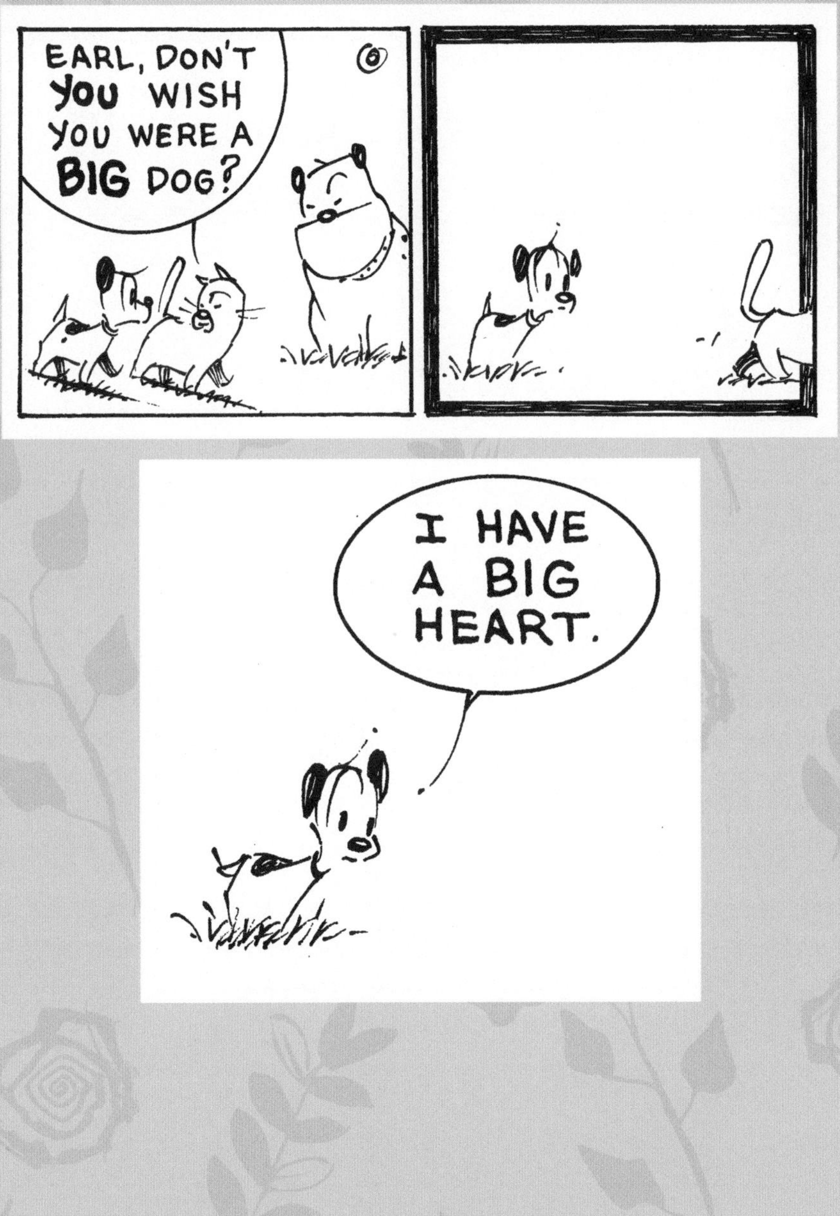
EARL, DON'T YOU WISH YOU WERE A BIG DOG?
I HAVE A BIG HEART.

I'VE DECIDED INSTEAD OF TRYING TO FIGHT ALL THE ILLS OF THE WORLD I WOULD JUST LOVE AND HUG EVERYTHING.
HOW RIDICULOUS! HOW NAIVE!!! HOW

...ABOUT THAT!?!

YOU LOOK LIKE YOU COULD USE A HUG.
I DO!?!

I DID.

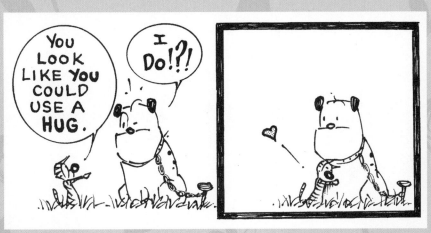

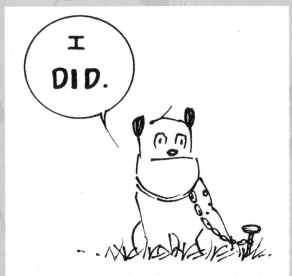

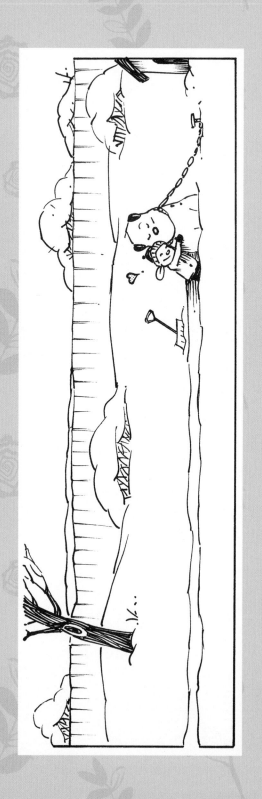

YOU CAN HELP YOUR LOCAL SHELTER BY VOLUNTEERING OR DONATING MONEY OR PET FOOD OR TOWELS, OR ANY ITEM ON THEIR WISH LIST.

I CAN DO THAT!

WHERE DO YOU KEEP YOUR DOG CHOW?

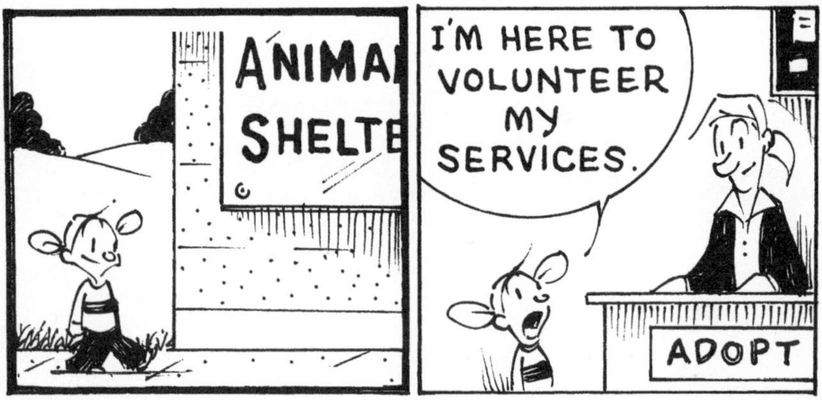
ANIMA
SHELTE
I'M HERE TO VOLUNTEER MY SERVICES.
ADOPT

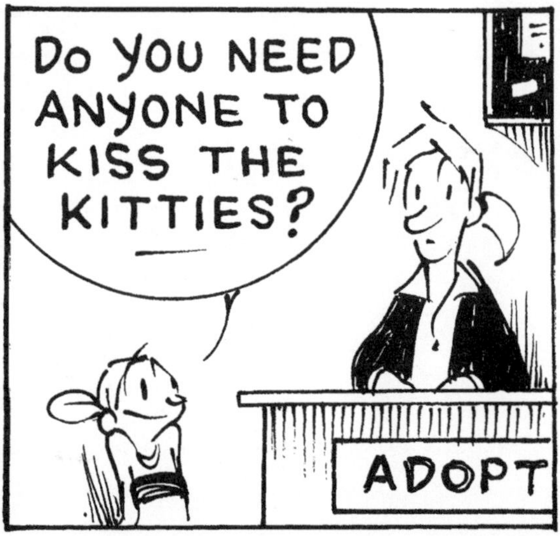
DO YOU NEED ANYONE TO KISS THE KITTIES?
ADOPT

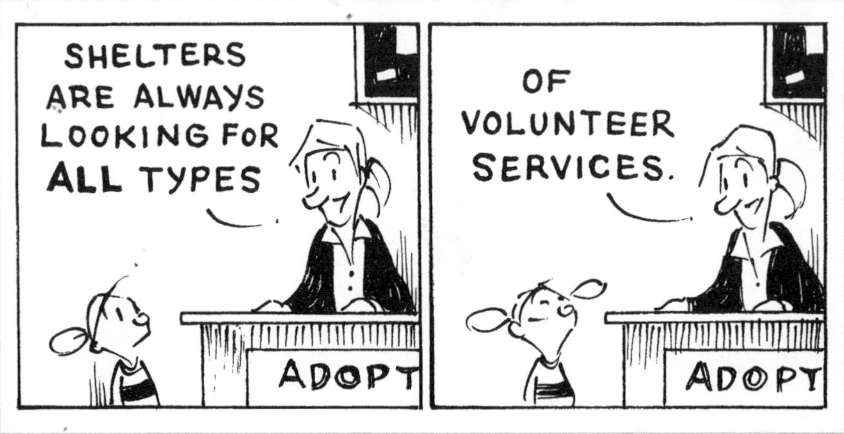
SHELTERS ARE ALWAYS LOOKING FOR ALL TYPES
ADOPT
OF VOLUNTEER SERVICES.
ADOPT

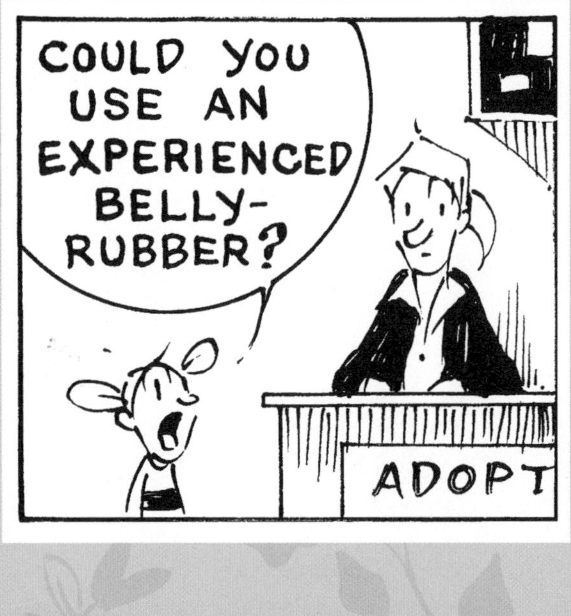
COULD YOU USE AN EXPERIENCED BELLY-RUBBER?
ADOPT

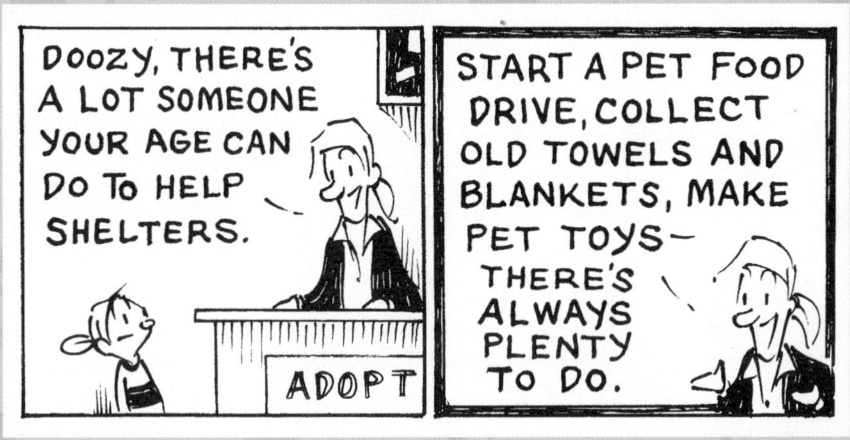
DOOZY, THERE'S A LOT SOMEONE YOUR AGE CAN DO TO HELP SHELTERS.
ADOPT
START A PET FOOD DRIVE, COLLECT OLD TOWELS AND BLANKETS, MAKE PET TOYS—
THERE'S ALWAYS PLENTY TO DO.

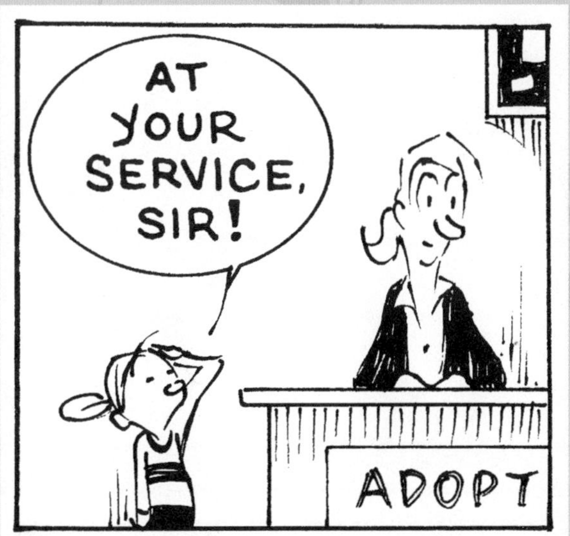
AT YOUR SERVICE, SIR!
ADOPT

ANIM
SHELT
WHAT'S DOOZY DOING?
SHE'S SERV-ING.
IS IT DINNER ALREADY?

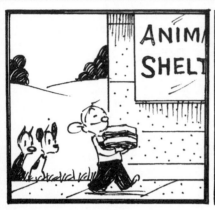

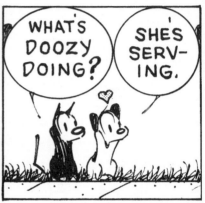

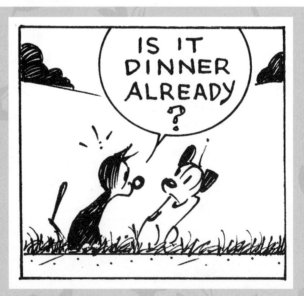

"No joy can equal
the joy of serving others."
~Sai Baba

It takes nothing away from a human
to be kind to an animal.

~ Joaquin Phoenix

*H*aving respect
for animals
makes us
better humans.

~ Jane Goodall

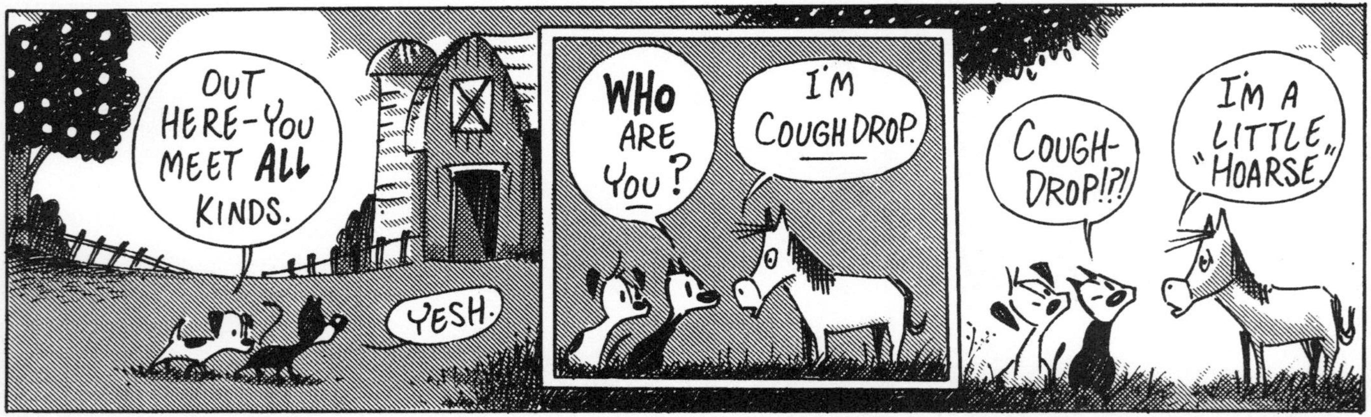
OUT HERE-YOU MEET **ALL** KINDS.
YESH.
WHO ARE YOU?
I'M COUGH DROP.
COUGH-DROP!?!
I'M A LITTLE "HOARSE."

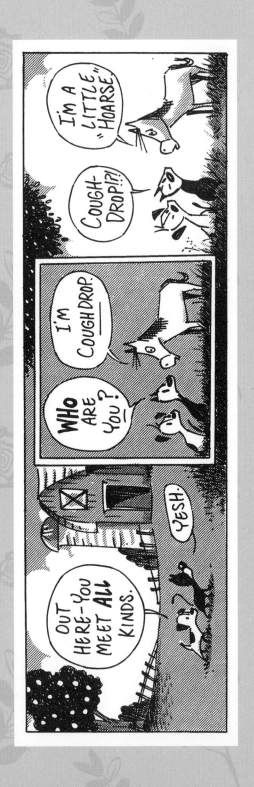

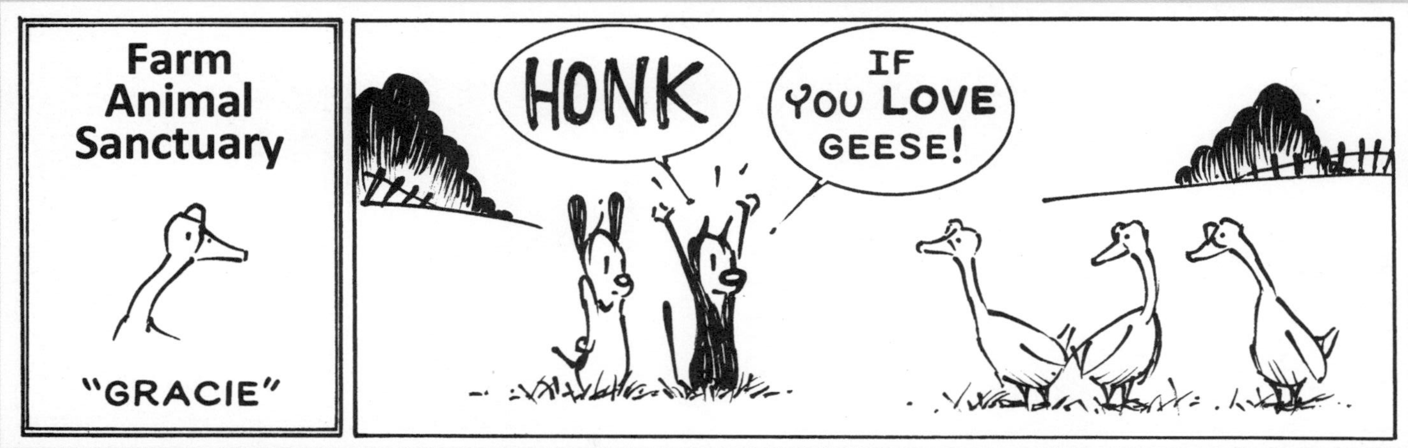
Farm Animal Sanctuary
"GRACIE"
HONK
IF YOU LOVE GEESE!

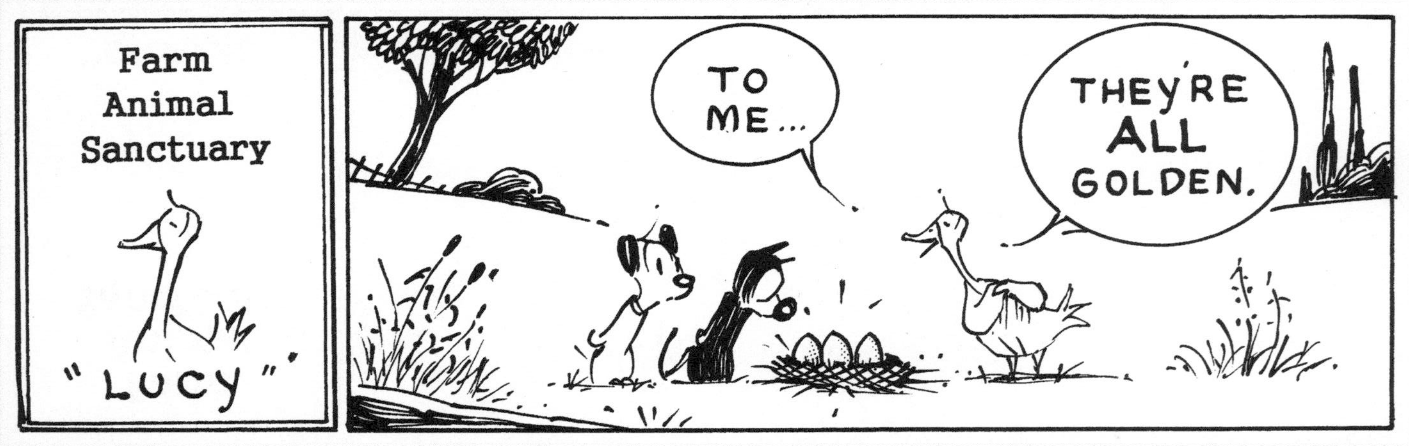
Farm
Animal
Sanctuary
"LUCY"
TO ME...
THEY'RE ALL GOLDEN.

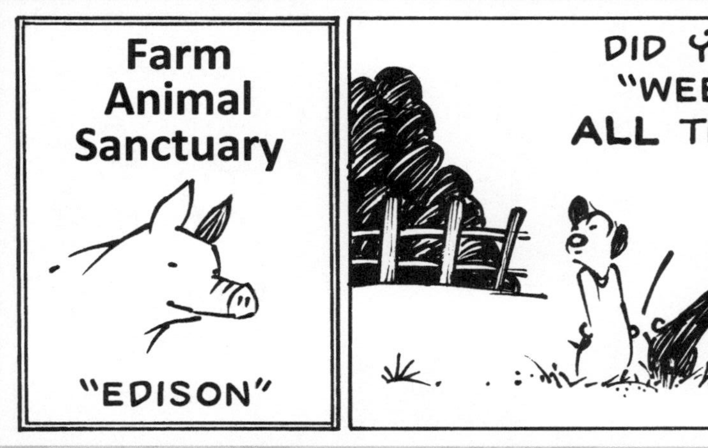
Farm
Animal
Sanctuary
"EDISON"
DID YOU EVER GO
"WEE-WEE-WEE"
ALL THE WAY HOME?

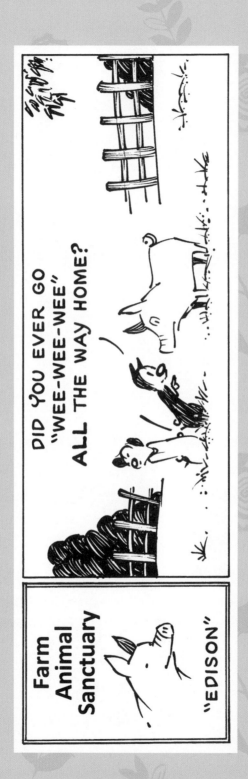

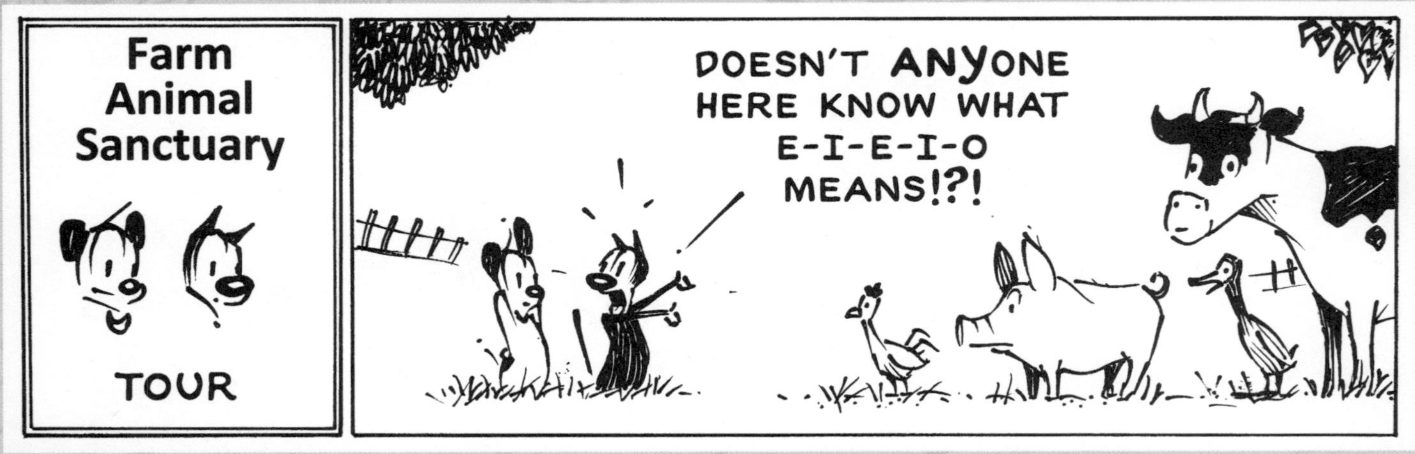
Farm Animal Sanctuary
TOUR
DOESN'T ANYONE HERE KNOW WHAT E-I-E-I-O MEANS!?!

IT WAS REAL NICE VISITING YOU AT THE FARM SANCTUARY, EDDIE!
NEXT TIME WE'LL BRING SOME FRIENDS.
GREAT.
MAKE SURE ONE IS AN APPLE.

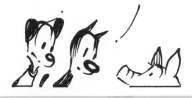

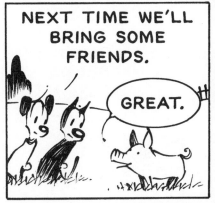

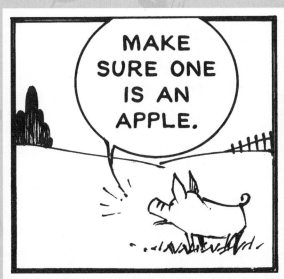

CLUCK CLUCK BOCK-A BOCK-A
BOCK-A BOCK BOCK-A CLUCK CLUCK
PARDON THE FOWL LANGUAGE.

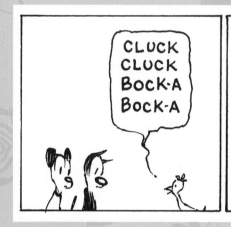

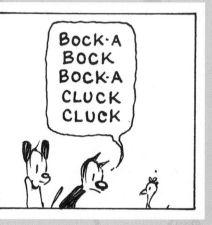

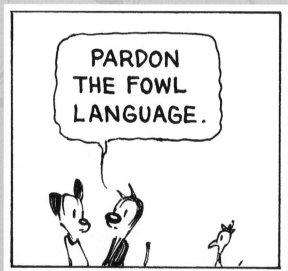

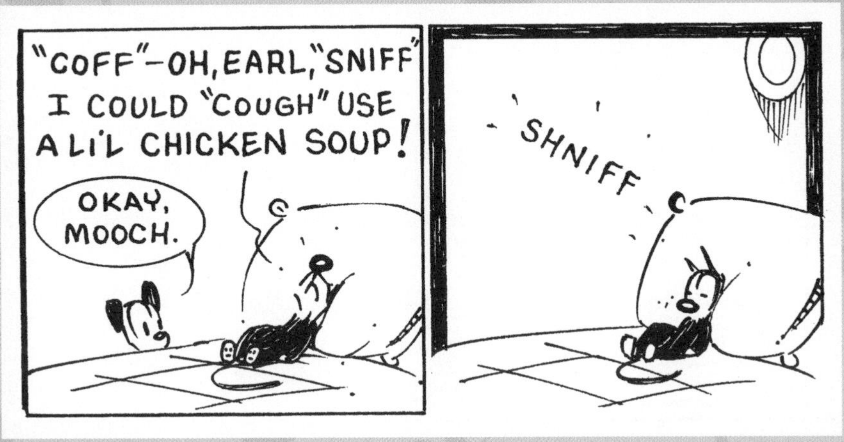
"COFF"-OH, EARL, "SNIFF" I COULD "COUGH" USE A LI'L CHICKEN SOUP!
OKAY, MOOCH.
SHNIFF

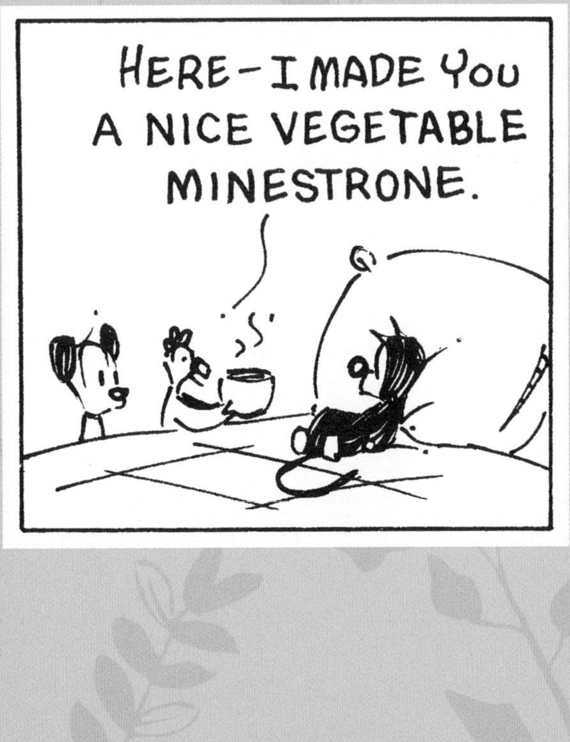
HERE-I MADE YOU A NICE VEGETABLE MINESTRONE.

TONIGHT, EARL- BROWN RICE, PEANUT BUTTER, BROCCOLI, AND CARROTS.
MEATLESS MONDAY.

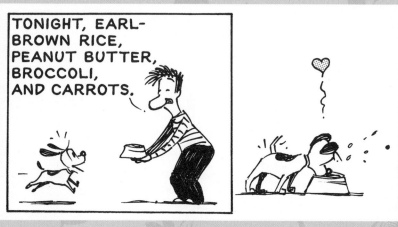

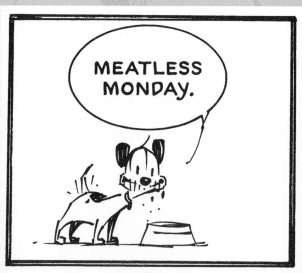

SMAK
SHMAK SMAK.
SMAK SHMAK
SMAK

ALWAYS KISS THE HAND THAT FEEDS YOU.

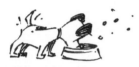

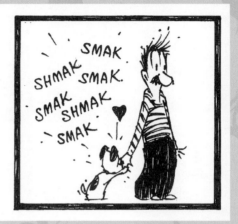

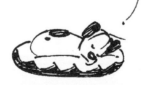

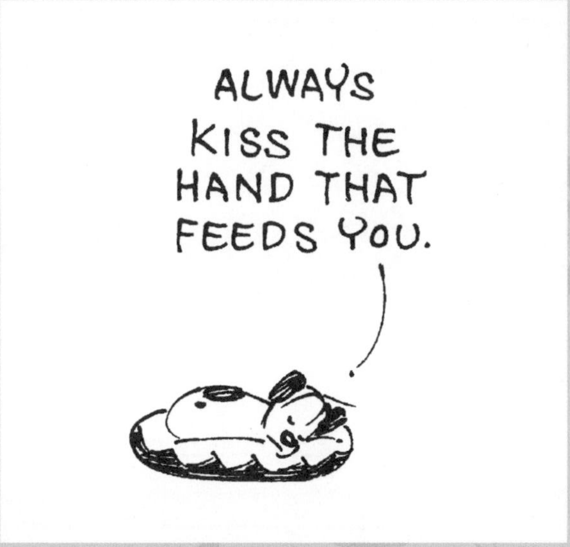

KNOCK KNOCK
SIR, DID YOU KNOW FACTORY FARMS NOT ONLY CAUSE SUFFERING FOR THE ANIMALS BUT ALSO HARM THE ENVIRON-MENT?
WOW.
PIGS ARE SMART.

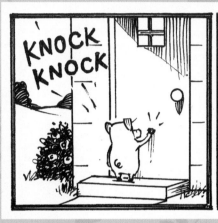

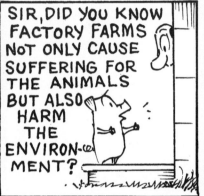

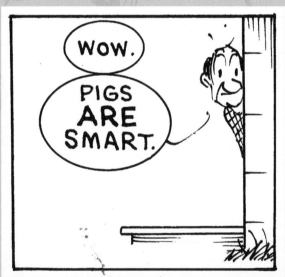

...AND NOW A LITTLE SONG: ♫ OL' MAC DONALD HAD A FACTORY FARM ♪ E·I·E·I·O
♫ AND ON HIS FARM HE HAD NO GRASS E·I·E·I·O ♫
♫ WITH NO GRASS HERE, NO SUNLIGHT THERE, JUST WIRE CAGES ♫ PILED UP EVERYWHERE
♫ CAN'T MOVE HERE, CAN'T MOVE THERE, CAN'T HARDLY EVEN BREATHE THE AIR ♫
♫ OL' MAC DONALD ♪ HAD A FACTORY FARM
E·I·E·I·OH!
THE REMAKE.

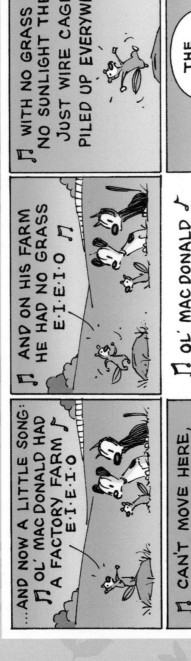

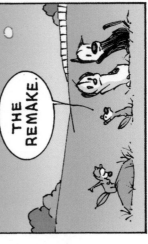

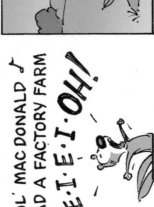

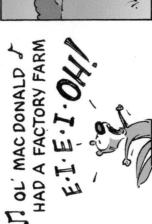

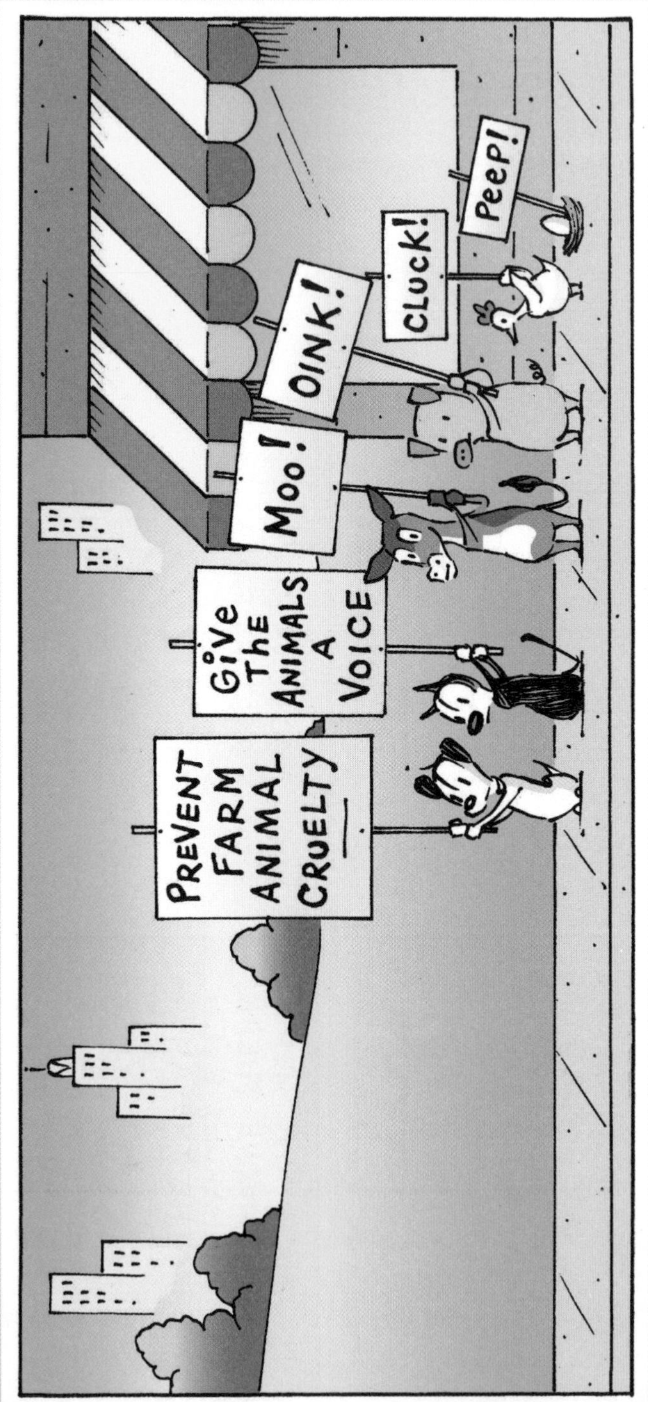
PREVENT FARM ANIMAL CRUELTY
GiVe The ANIMALS A VOICE
Moo!
OINK!
CLUCK!
PeeP!

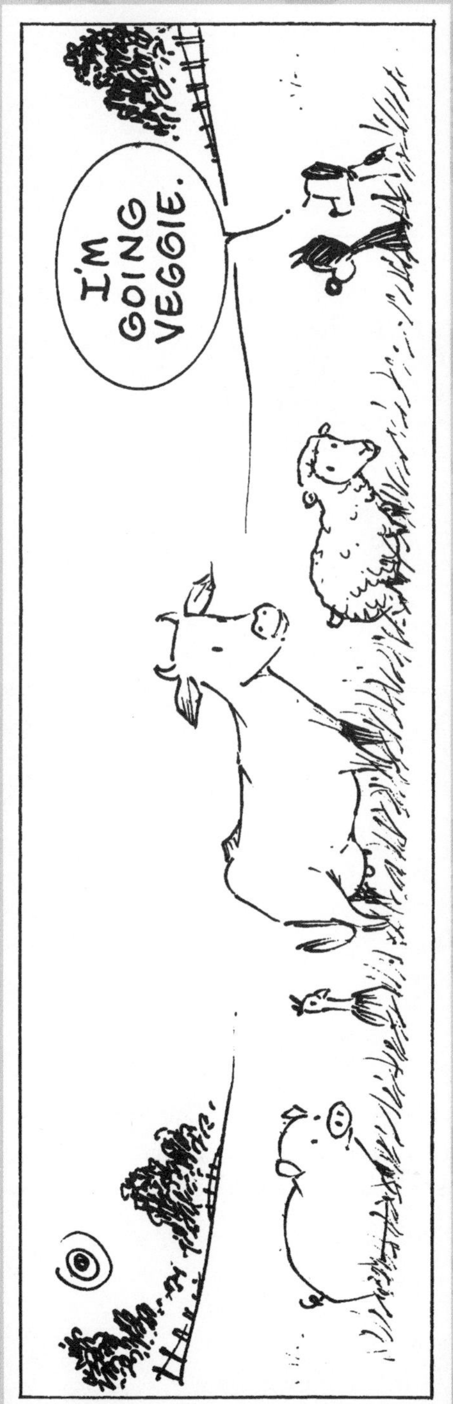
I'M GOING VEGGIE.

BUTCHIE'S GONE VEGGIE!
FATTY SNAX DELI
NOW PLANT-BASED
OPEN

NO BULL?
...OR PORK, OR CHICKEN!

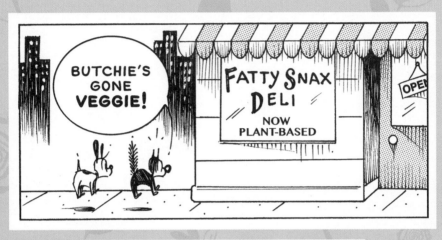

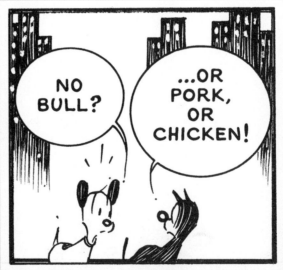

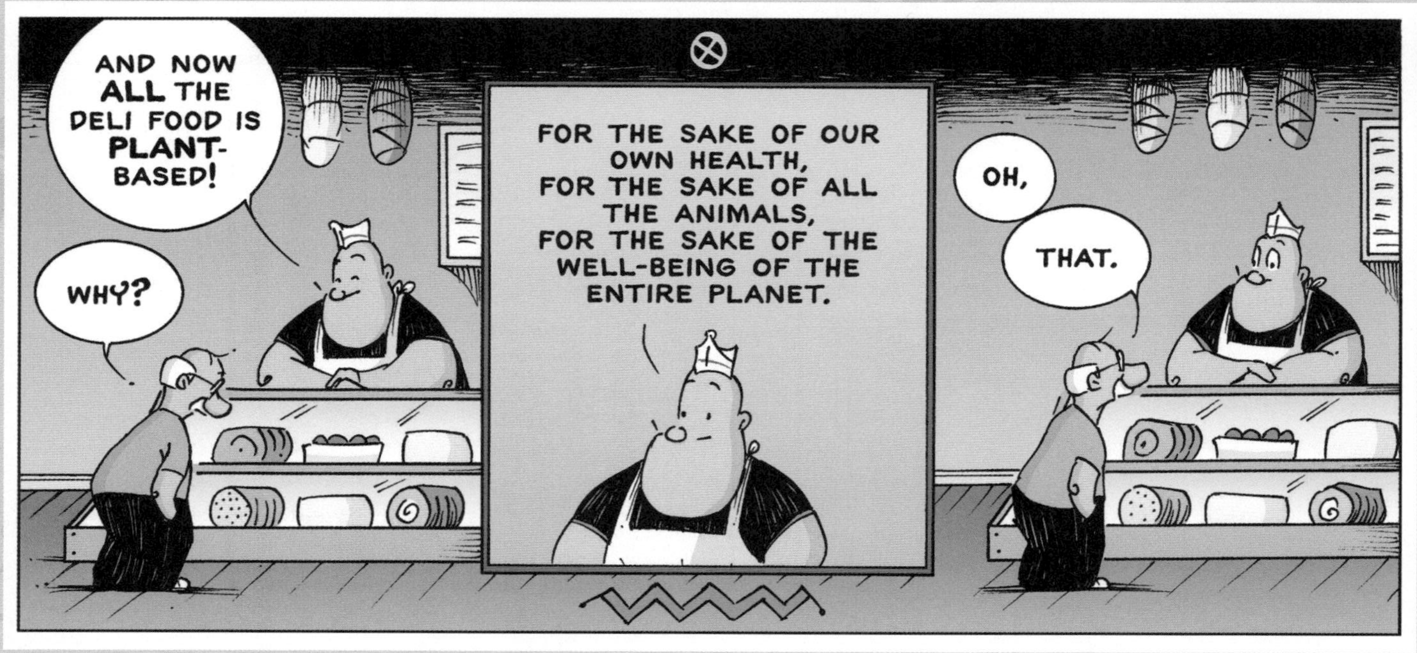
AND NOW ALL THE DELI FOOD IS PLANT-BASED!
WHY?
FOR THE SAKE OF OUR OWN HEALTH, FOR THE SAKE OF ALL THE ANIMALS, FOR THE SAKE OF THE WELL-BEING OF THE ENTIRE PLANET.
OH,
THAT.

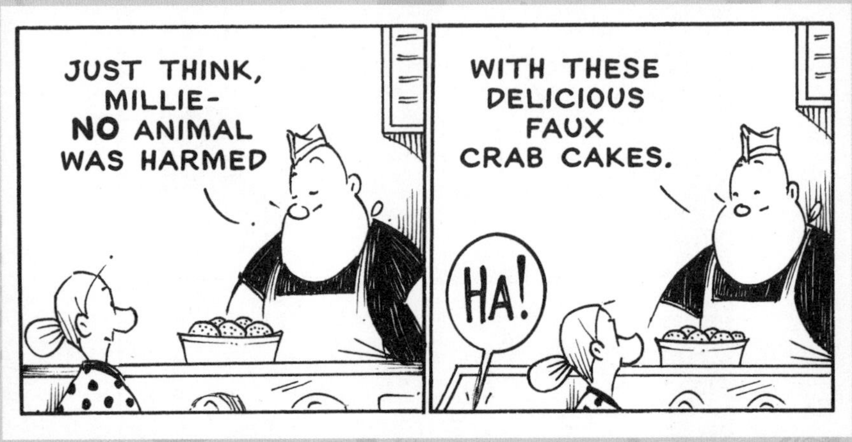
JUST THINK, MILLIE- **NO** ANIMAL WAS HARMED
WITH THESE DELICIOUS FAUX CRAB CAKES.
HA!

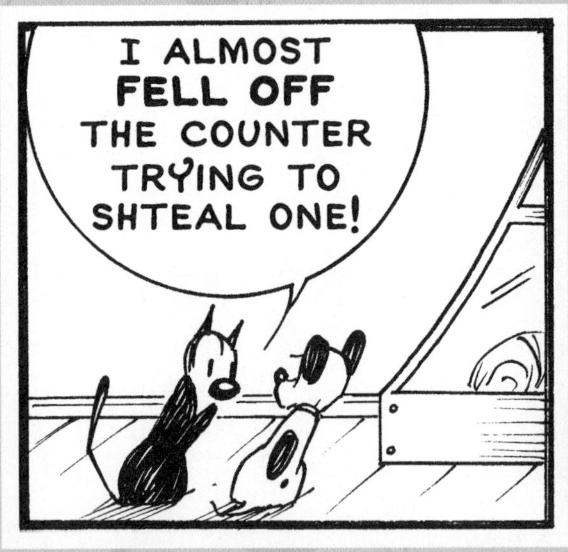
I ALMOST **FELL OFF** THE COUNTER TRYING TO SHTEAL ONE!

I'M NOT SURE I CAN **DO** THIS.
TAKE LITTLE STEPS. EVERYTHING HELPS. HERE, TRY A **VEGAN** CUPCAKE.
CHOMP CHOMP

MAY I TAKE ANOTHER STEP?

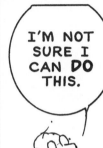

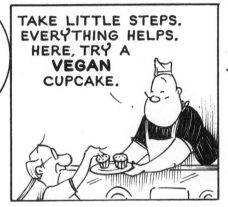

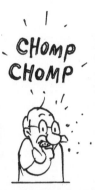

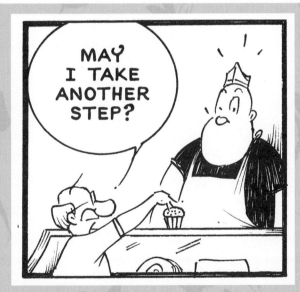

Nothing will benefit human health and increase the chances for survival of life on Earth as much as the evolution to a vegetarian diet.

-Albert Einstein

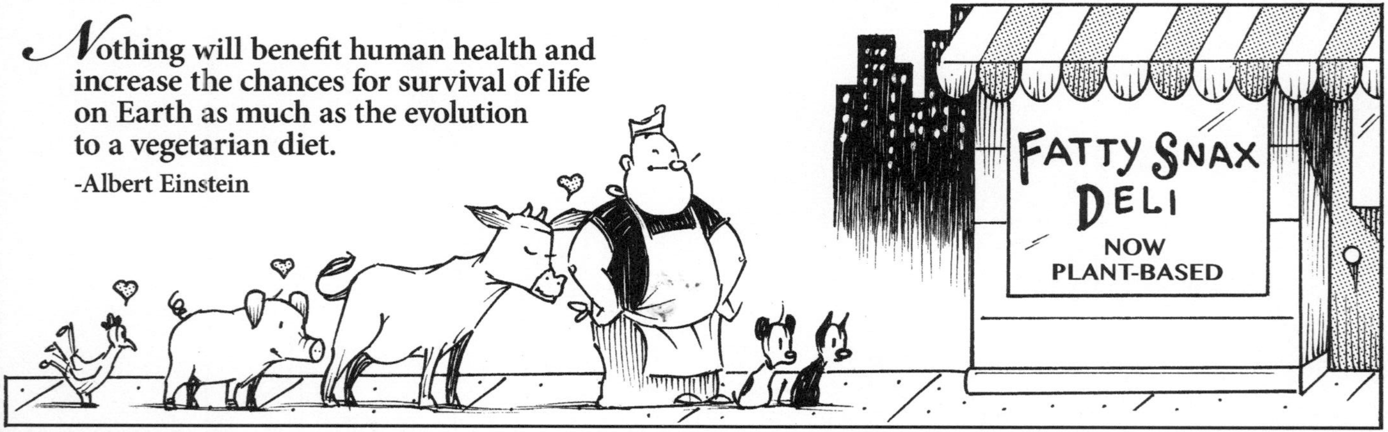
FATTY SNAX
DELI
NOW
PLANT-BASED

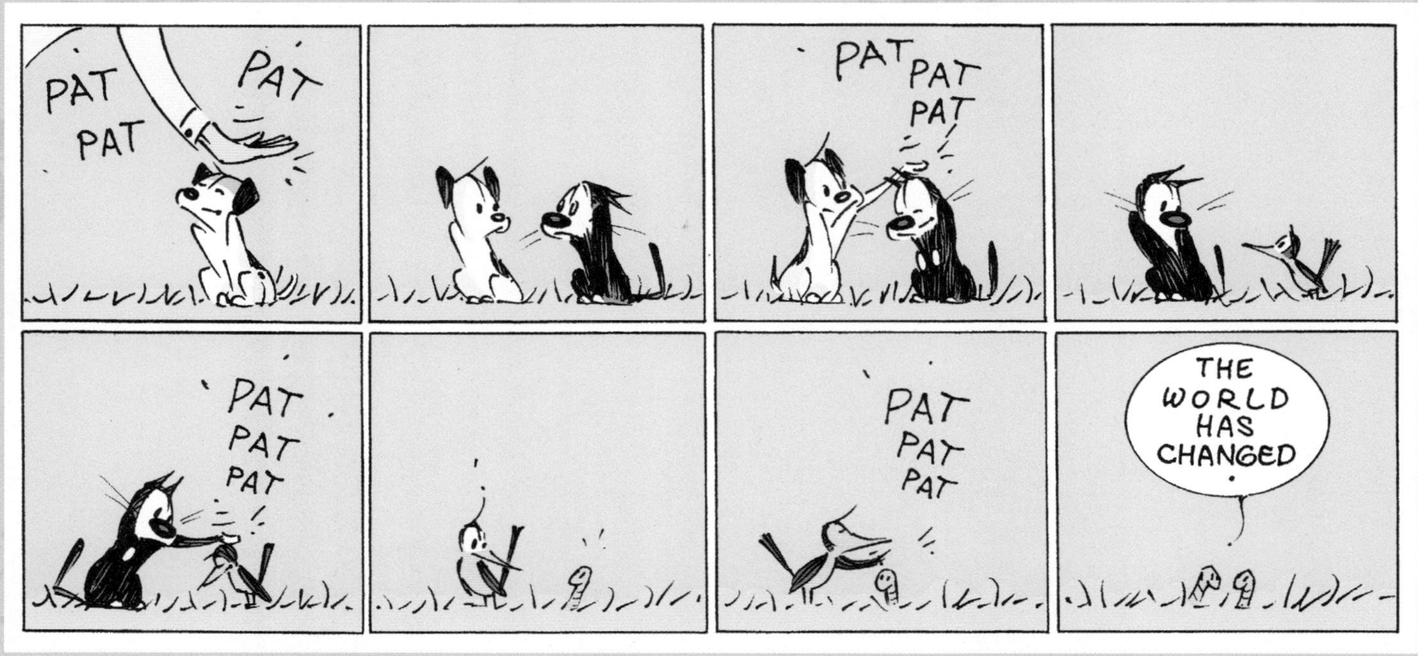
PAT
PAT
PAT
PAT PAT PAT
PAT
PAT
PAT
PAT
PAT
PAT
THE WORLD HAS CHANGED.

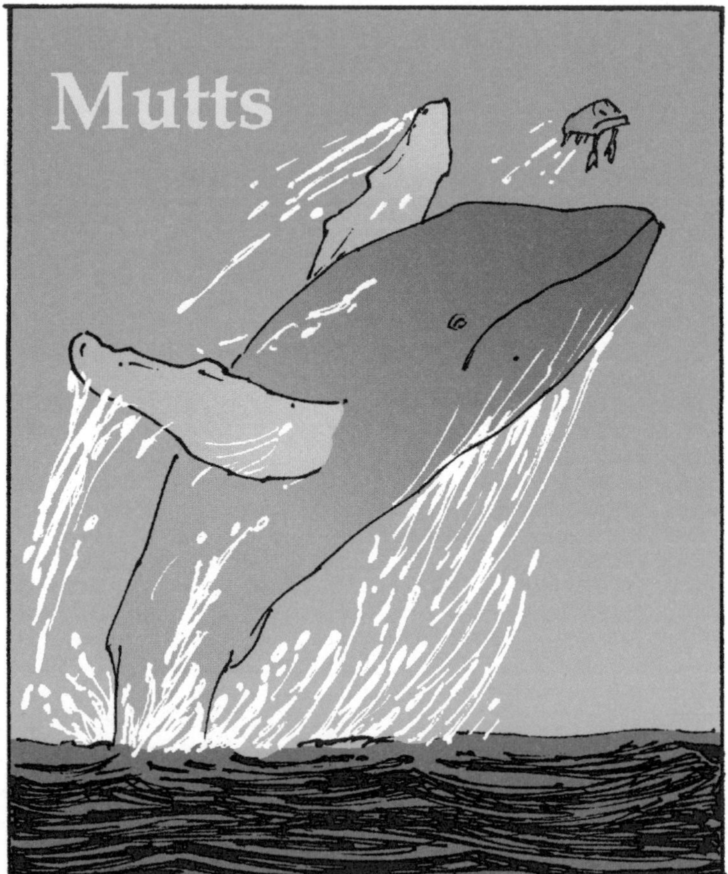
Mutts

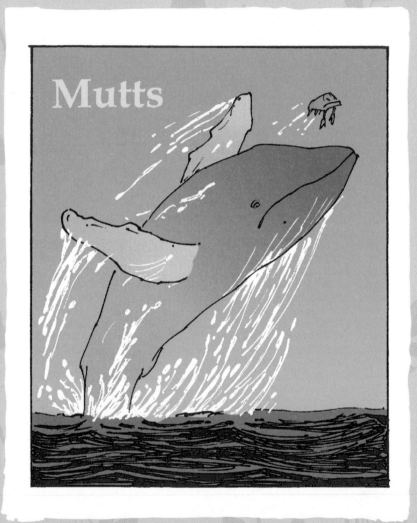

Keep It CLEAN

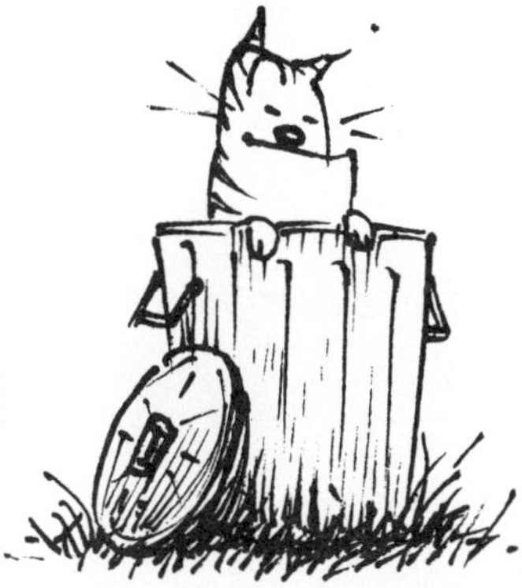

The earth is the only planet in the solar system known to support life. That's because it has two things in abundance that living beings need to survive: air and water. Our planet is beautiful but also fragile, and it's everyone's job to keep it clean and healthy.

Think for a minute about everything that is wasted. Americans send over 200 million tons of garbage to landfills each year, with millions more ending up in our oceans. We believe things can be "thrown away," but where do thrown-away things go? They are still here, on land and adrift in our seas. Ninety percent of all our plastic waste has never been recycled. Plastic bottles take 450 years to decompose in a landfill, and other plastics can remain intact for 1,000 years. Our oceans can be sustainable, but we must leave the fish in the sea and stop throwing plastic "away."

If we use less, there will be less to recycle or discard. Refuse to accept things like single-use plastics (such as straws and plastic wrapping). Some are not needed at all, while others can be replaced with reusable versions. If you can't use something, give it to someone who can, or recycle it. This prevents pollution, saves energy, and—like eating less meat—reduces greenhouse gases, which will help keep the planet cool, green, and clean.

Hopefully, if you watch SpongeBob, *you see plankton and crabs and starfish—and you'll (want to) take care of our oceans.*

—Stephen Hillenburg, creator of *SpongeBob SquarePants*

How to Keep It Clean

- Unplug. Turn off lights and electronic devices when you aren't using them.

- Save water—don't waste it! Turn off the faucet whenever you can, like when you are brushing your teeth.

- Don't waste food—leftovers are delicious!

- Look for things you need at yard sales or thrift shops.

- If you bring your lunch with you, wrap it in something that can be reused or recycled.

- Reject single-use plastics like plastic straws and plastic wrap.

- Avoid using pesticides. Bugs pollinate plants.

- Compost. Turn food waste into organic material to help plants grow, keeping waste out of landfills.

- Look for things made of already recycled materials.

- Volunteer to help clean up your local park or beach.

- Recycle paper you no longer need.

- Donate your old toys and clothes.

- Use refillable water bottles.

- Don't litter.

- Buy less stuff.

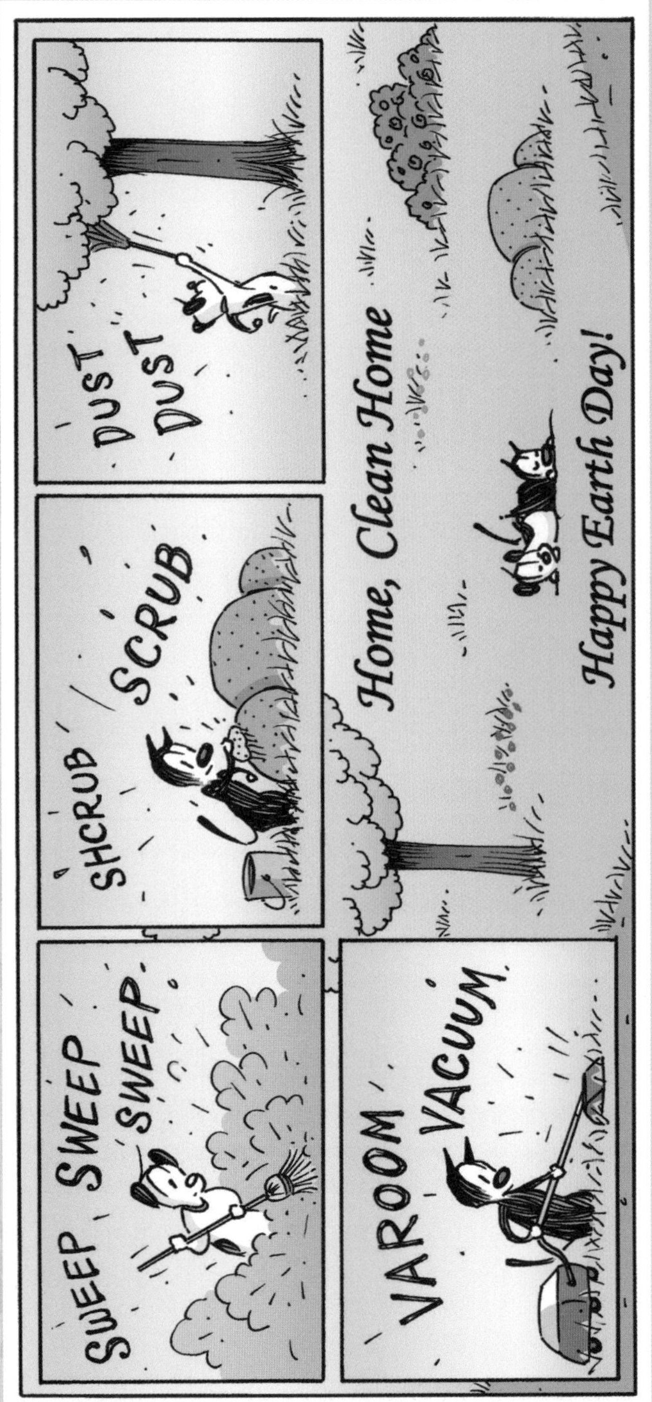
SWEEP SWEEP SWEEP
SHCRUB SCRUB
DUST DUST
VAROOM VACUUM
Home, Clean Home
Happy Earth Day!

SHTINKY'S TO·DO LIST...
TO HELP STOP GLOBAL WARMING —
1. STAY COOL

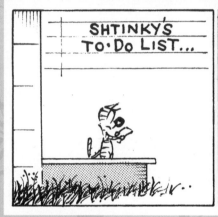

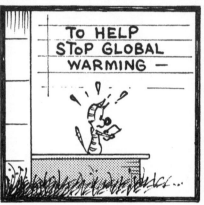

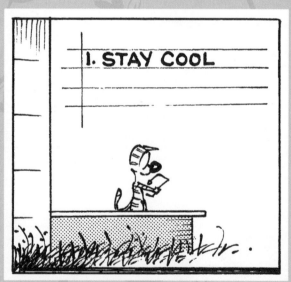

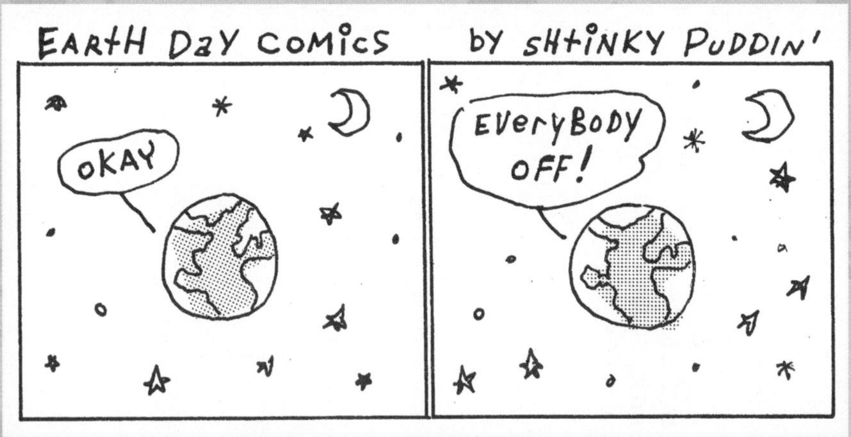
EARTH DAY COMICS
BY SHTINKY PUDDIN'
OKAY
EVERYBODY OFF!

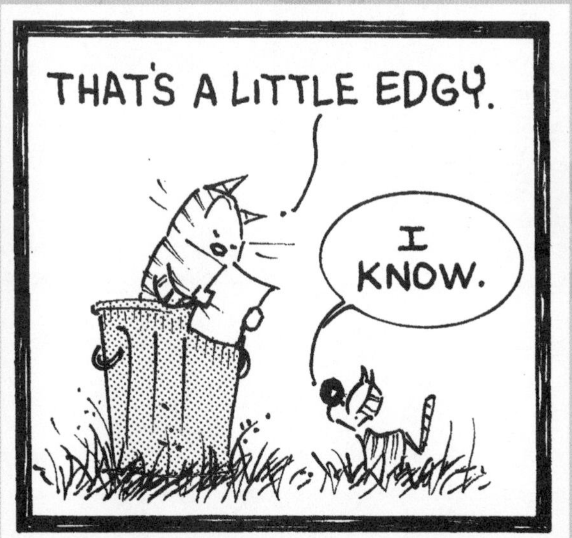
THAT'S A LITTLE EDGY.
I KNOW.

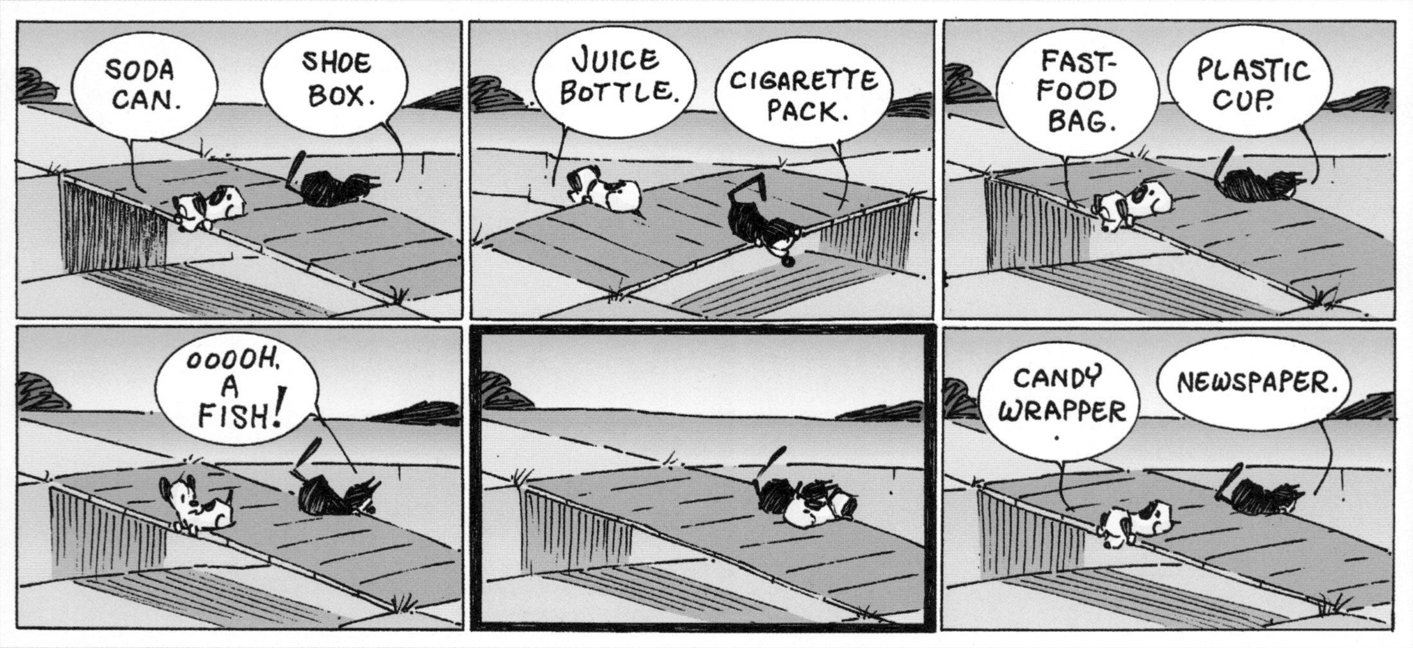

SODA CAN.
SHOE BOX.
JUICE BOTTLE.
CIGARETTE PACK.
FAST-FOOD BAG.
PLASTIC CUP.
OOOOH, A FISH!
CANDY WRAPPER.
NEWSPAPER.

HELLO THERE.
EEEEK!
I'M TAKING A BATH!

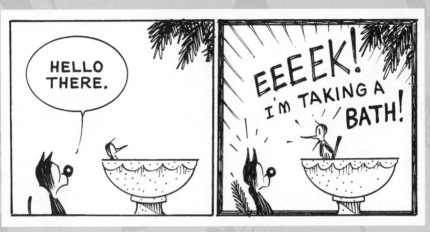

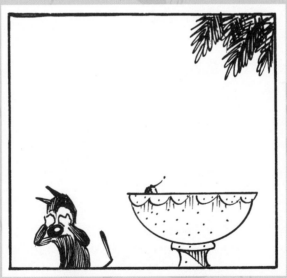

DON'T YOU LIKE BIRD BATHS?
I PREFER SHOWERS.

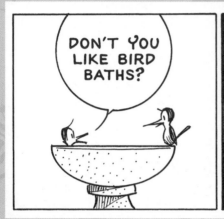

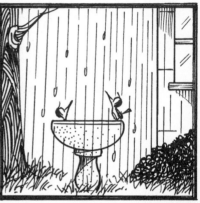

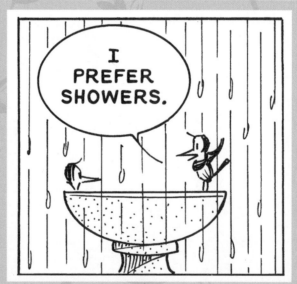

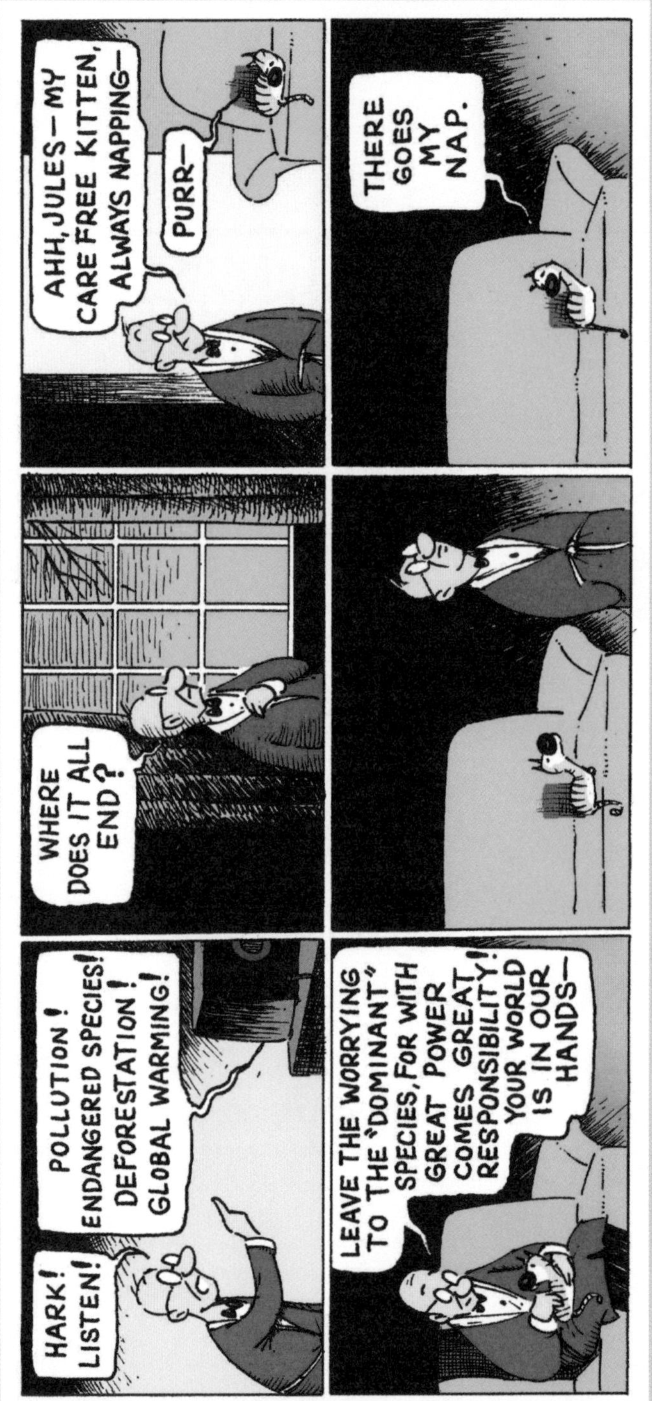
HARK! LISTEN!
POLLUTION! ENDANGERED SPECIES! DEFORESTATION! GLOBAL WARMING!
WHERE DOES IT ALL END?
AHH, JULES—MY CAREFREE KITTEN, ALWAYS NAPPING—
PURR—
LEAVE THE WORRYING TO THE "DOMINANT" SPECIES, FOR WITH GREAT POWER COMES GREAT RESPONSIBILITY! YOUR WORLD IS IN OUR HANDS—
THERE GOES MY NAP.

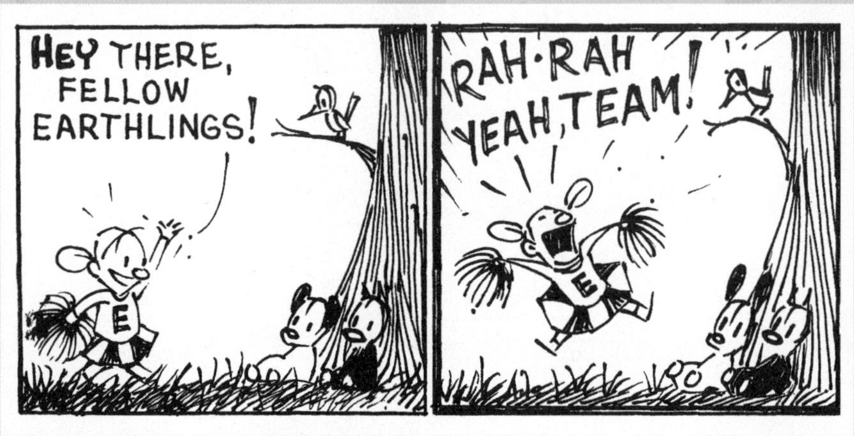
HEY THERE, FELLOW EARTHLINGS!
RAH·RAH YEAH, TEAM!

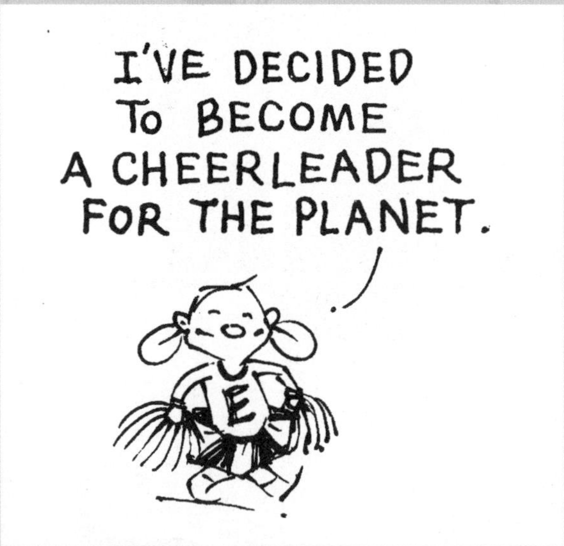
I'VE DECIDED TO BECOME A CHEERLEADER FOR THE PLANET.

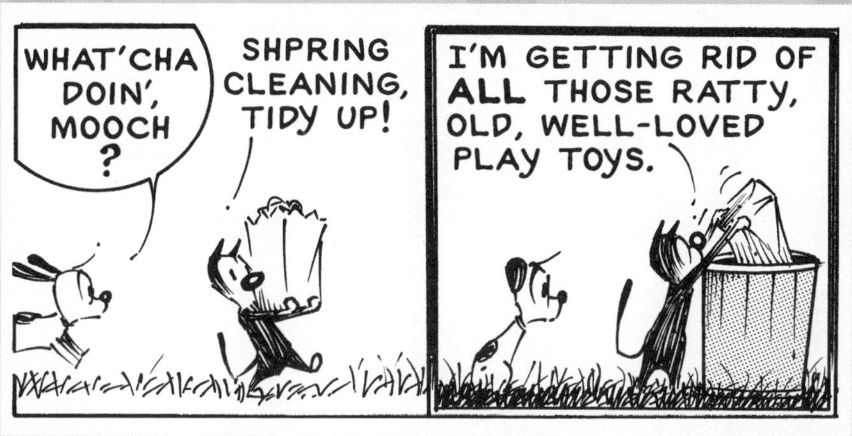
WHAT'CHA DOIN', MOOCH ?
SHPRING CLEANING, TIDY UP!
I'M GETTING RID OF ALL THOSE RATTY, OLD, WELL-LOVED PLAY TOYS.

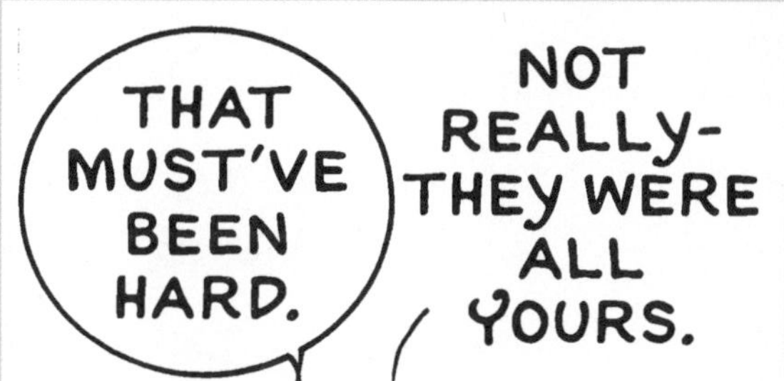
THAT MUST'VE BEEN HARD.
NOT REALLY- THEY WERE ALL YOURS.

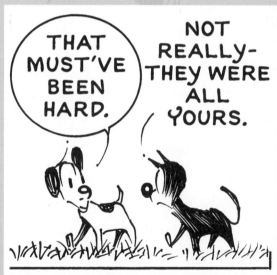

BONK
COULD YOU TOSS THAT BACK UP TO ME ?
I LIKE TO RECYCLE

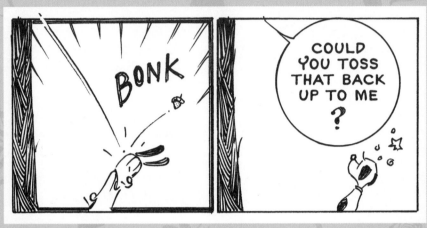

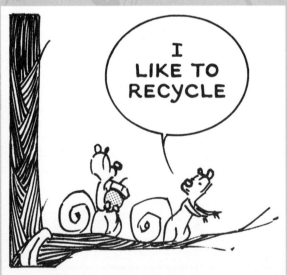

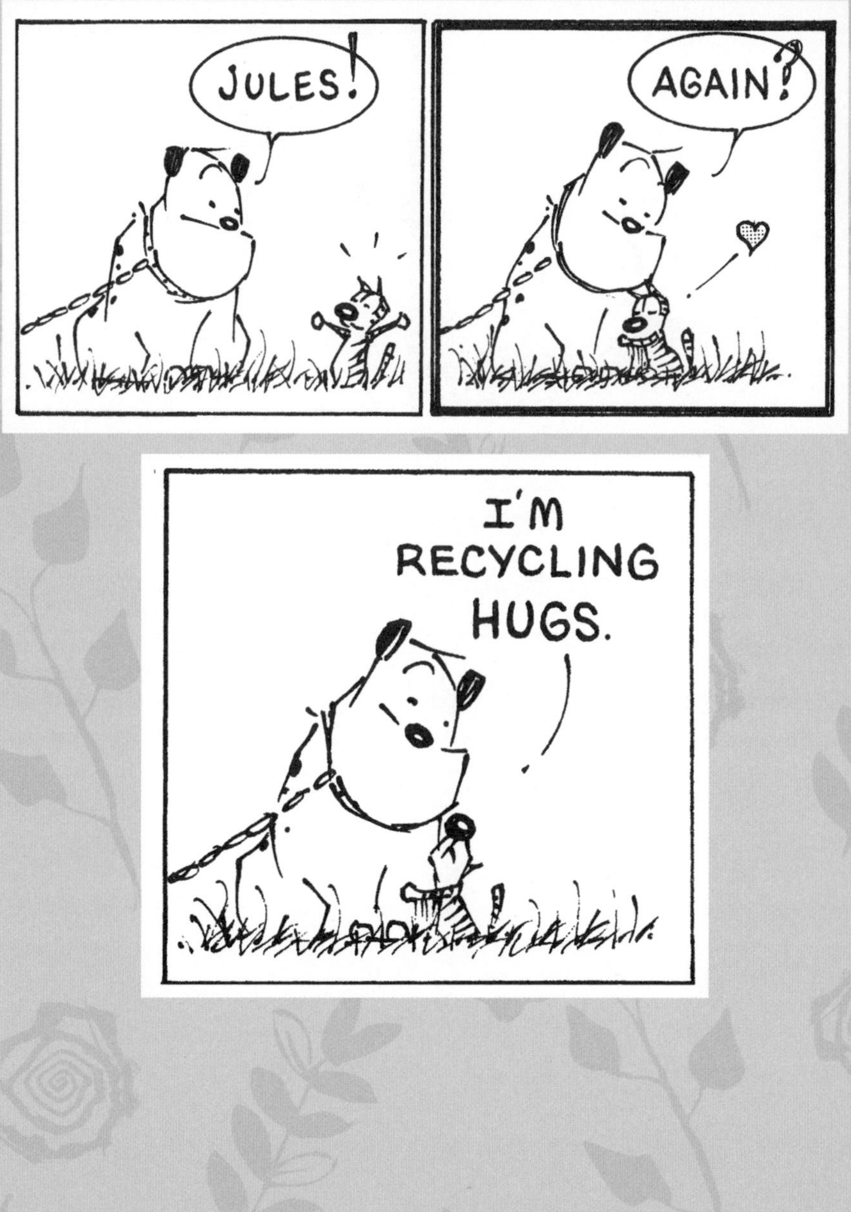
JULES!
AGAIN?!
I'M RECYCLING HUGS.

THINGS HAPPEN.

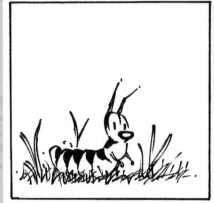

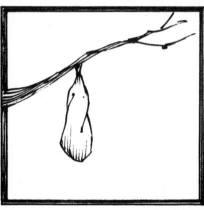

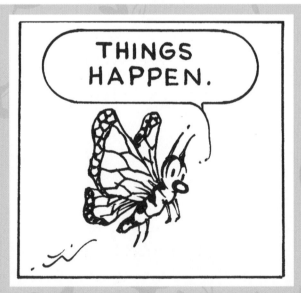

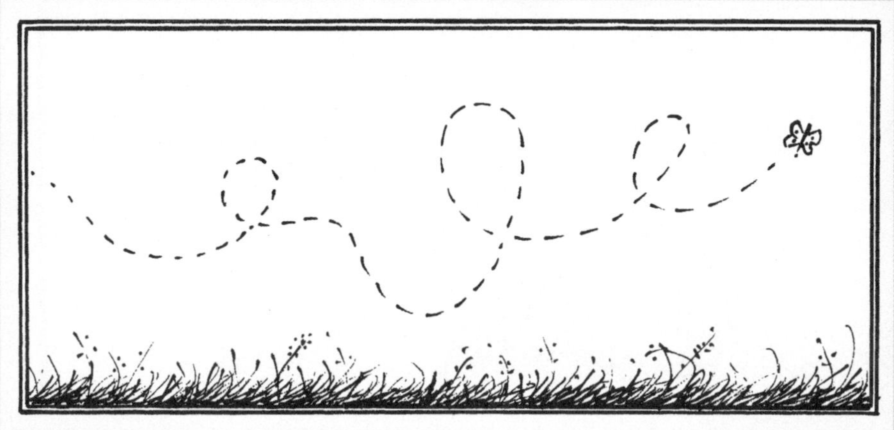

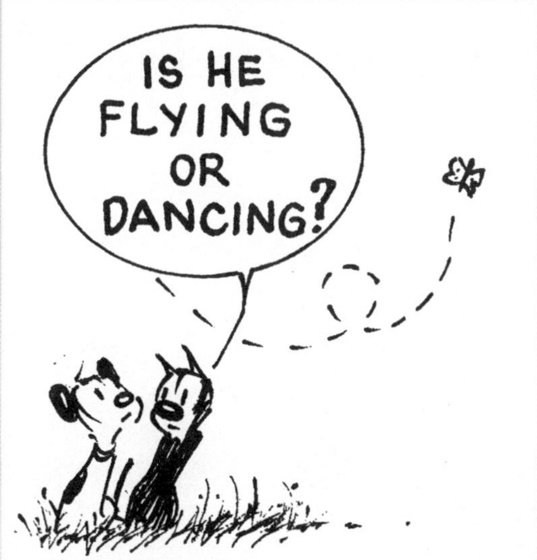
IS HE FLYING OR DANCING?

BEES ARE **ESSENTIAL** TO OUR ECOSYSTEM.
BUT MANY ARE DISAPPEARING DUE IN PART TO HARMFUL PESTICIDES.
UGH. I SAY...
LET THEM BEE!

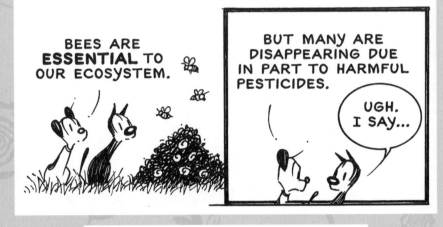

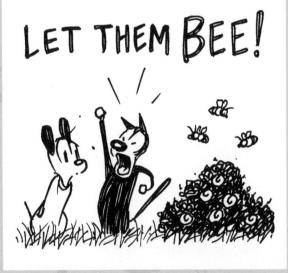

EARL, D'YA THINK WE'LL EVER BE INVADED BY CREATURES WHO'D DESTROY OUR PLANET WITH ALIEN TECHNOLOGY?
NAH. THAT'S JUST SCI-FI HOOEY!
LAWN SPRAY
OOFAH!
THE TRUTH IS OUT THERE.
YESH.

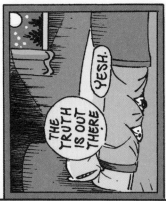

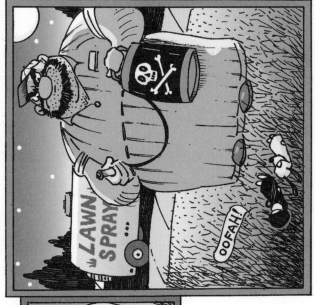

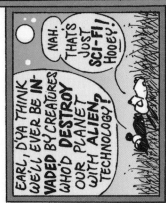

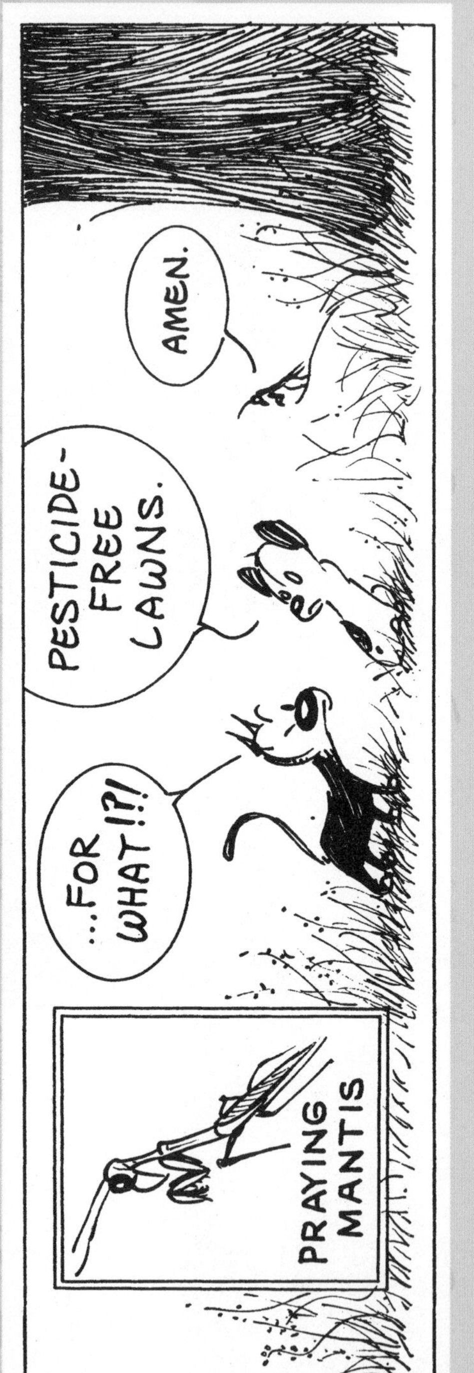
PRAYING MANTIS
...FOR WHAT!?!
PESTICIDE-FREE LAWNS.
AMEN.

WHEN BIRD-WATCHING, YOU NEVER KNOW WHAT YOU MIGHT SEE...
WOW! A PESTICIDE-FREE SUBURBAN LAWN!
NOWADAYS— THAT'S A RARE SIGHTING.

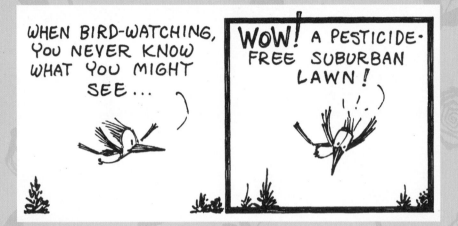

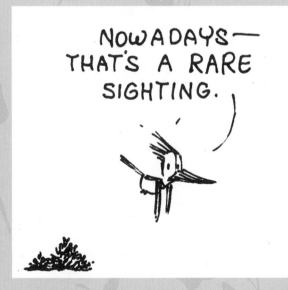

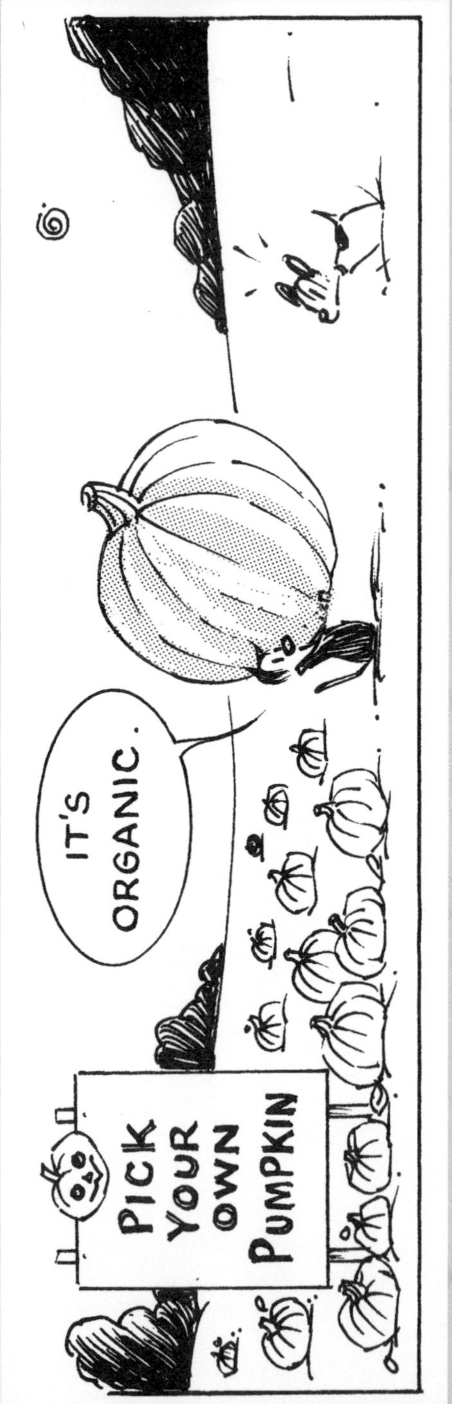
PICK YOUR OWN PUMPKIN
IT'S ORGANIC.

SO, EARL, HOW DO YOU LIKE DOOZY'S ELECTRIC BOBBIE DOLL CAR?
NICE
WOW! LISTEN TO THAT ENGINE PURR!
I THINK THAT'S ME.

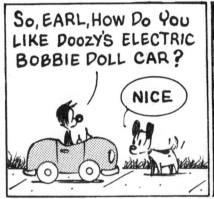

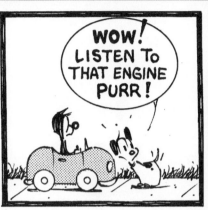

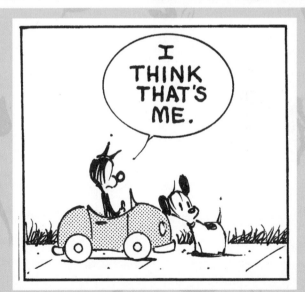

MY CAR RUNS ON ELECTRIC BATTERY
AND KITTY TREATS
IT'S A HYBRID.

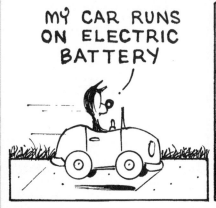

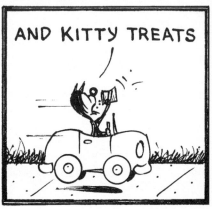

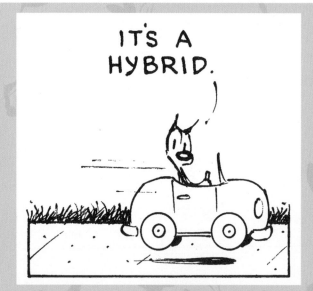

CRABBY— DID YOU EVER SEE A SEA MONSTER !?!
YES!
IT WAS A HIDEOUS BEHEMOTH OF A BEAST, LEAVING BEHIND A PATH OF WANTON DESTRUCTION AND SORROW!
DID IT BREATHE FIRE?
YOW!
No.
IT SPILLED OIL.

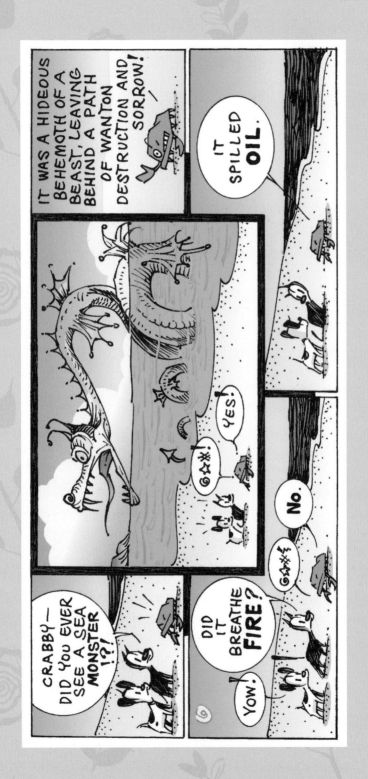

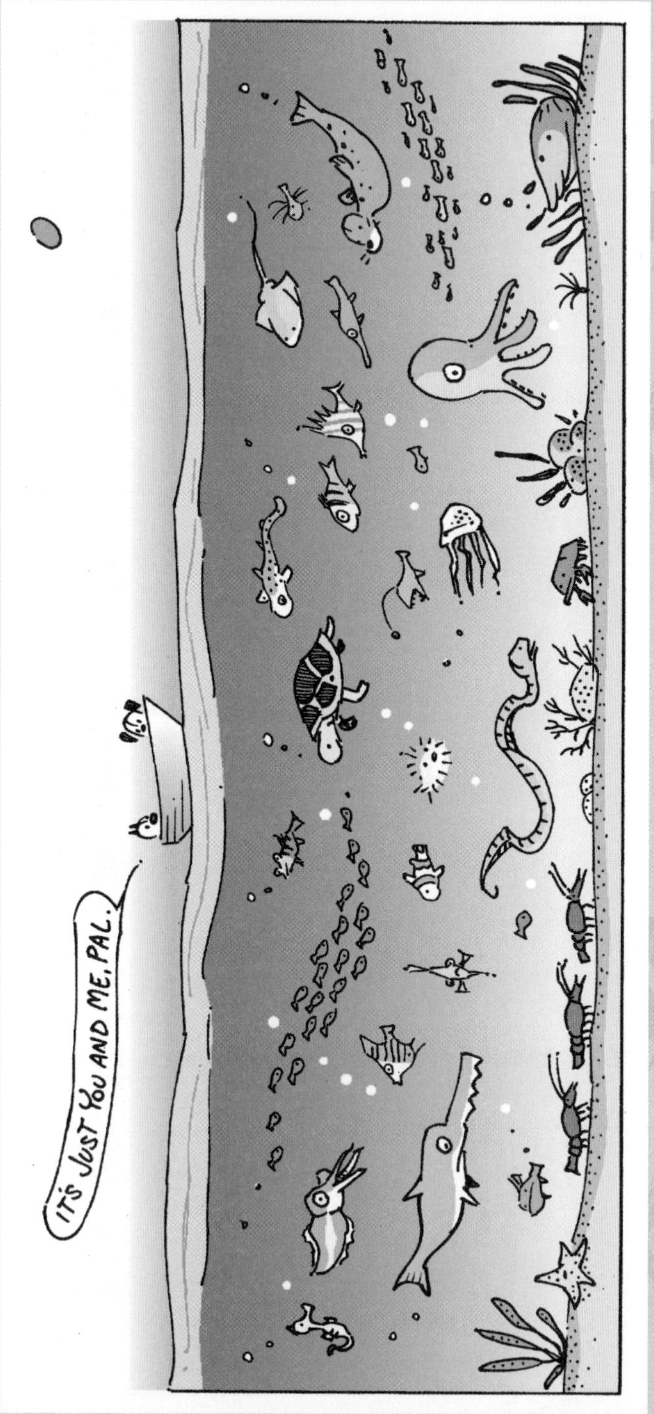
IT'S JUST YOU AND ME, PAL.

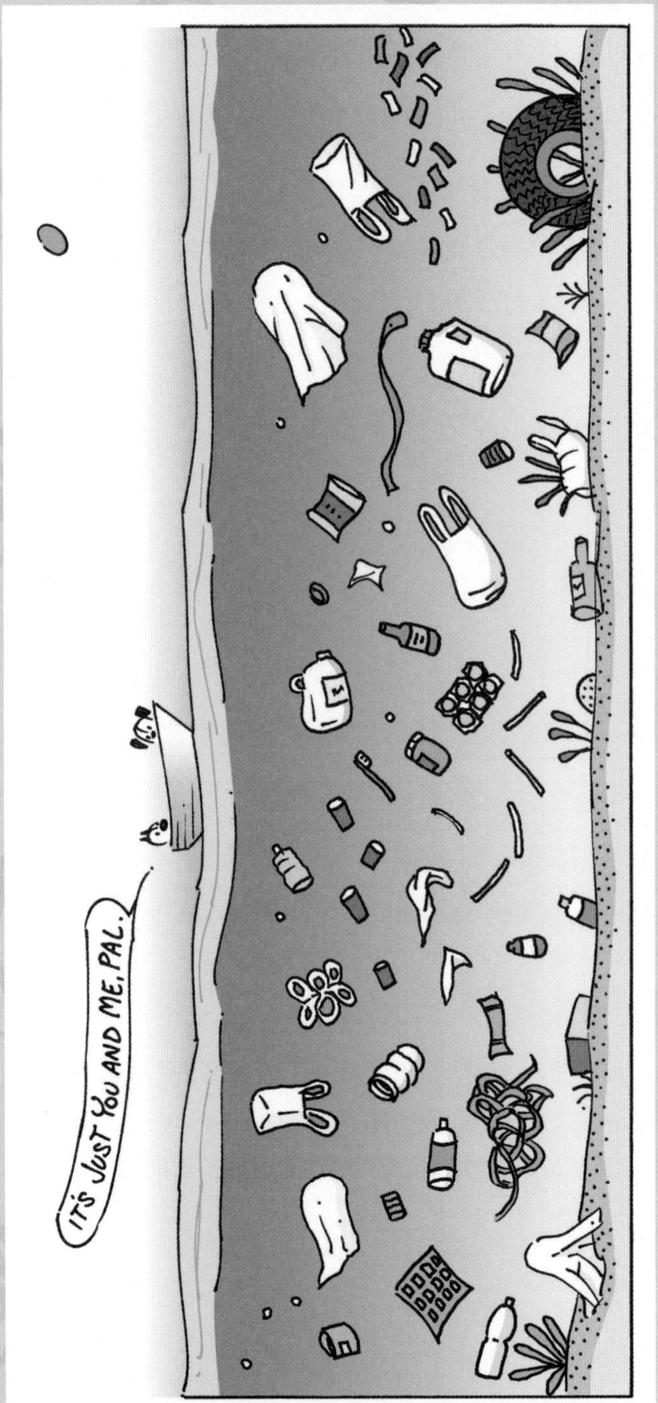
IT'S JUST YOU AND ME, PAL.

WE'VE BEEN ON THE BEACH ALL MORNING COLLECTING
SEA-SHELLS?
©
PLASTIC

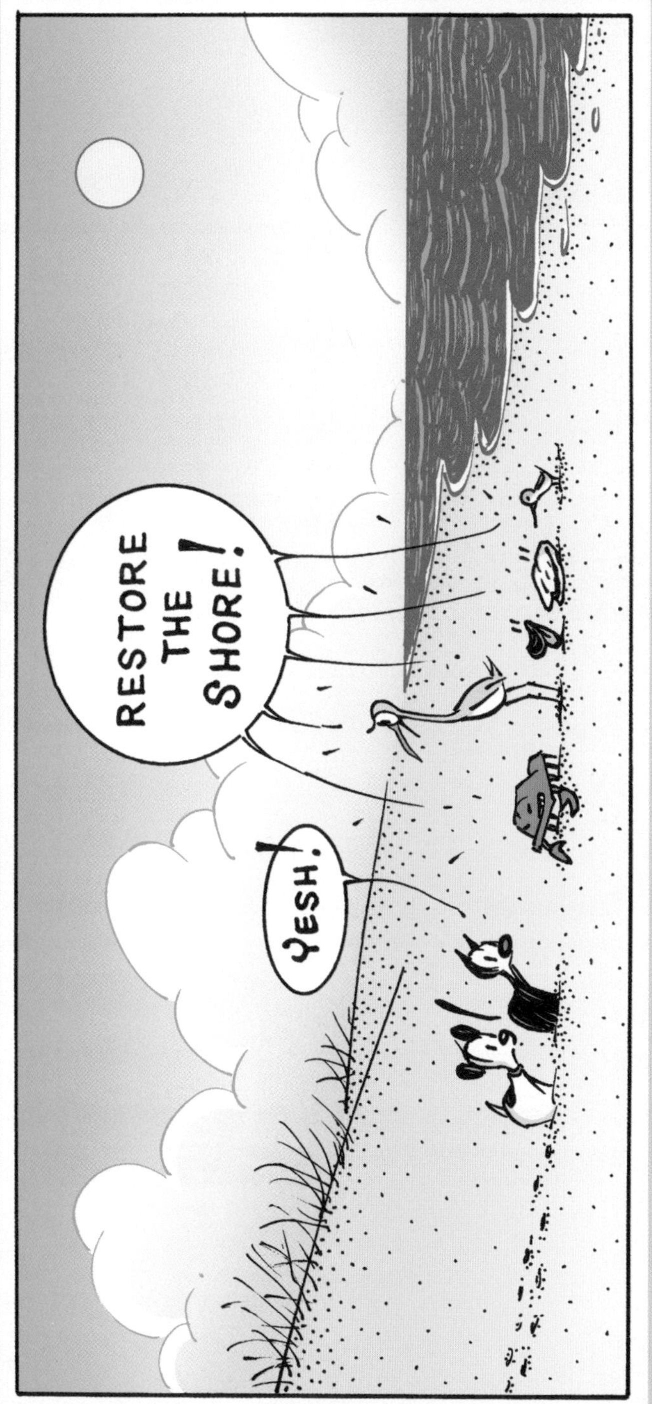
RESTORE THE SHORE!
YESH!

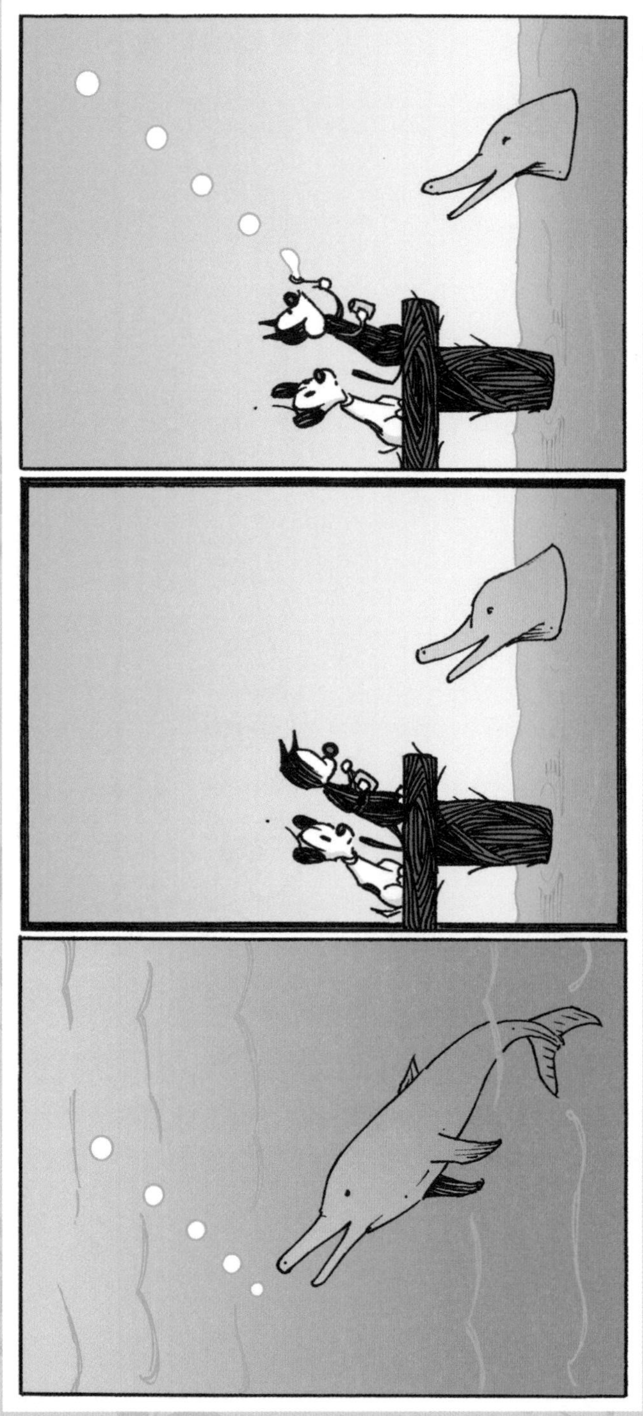

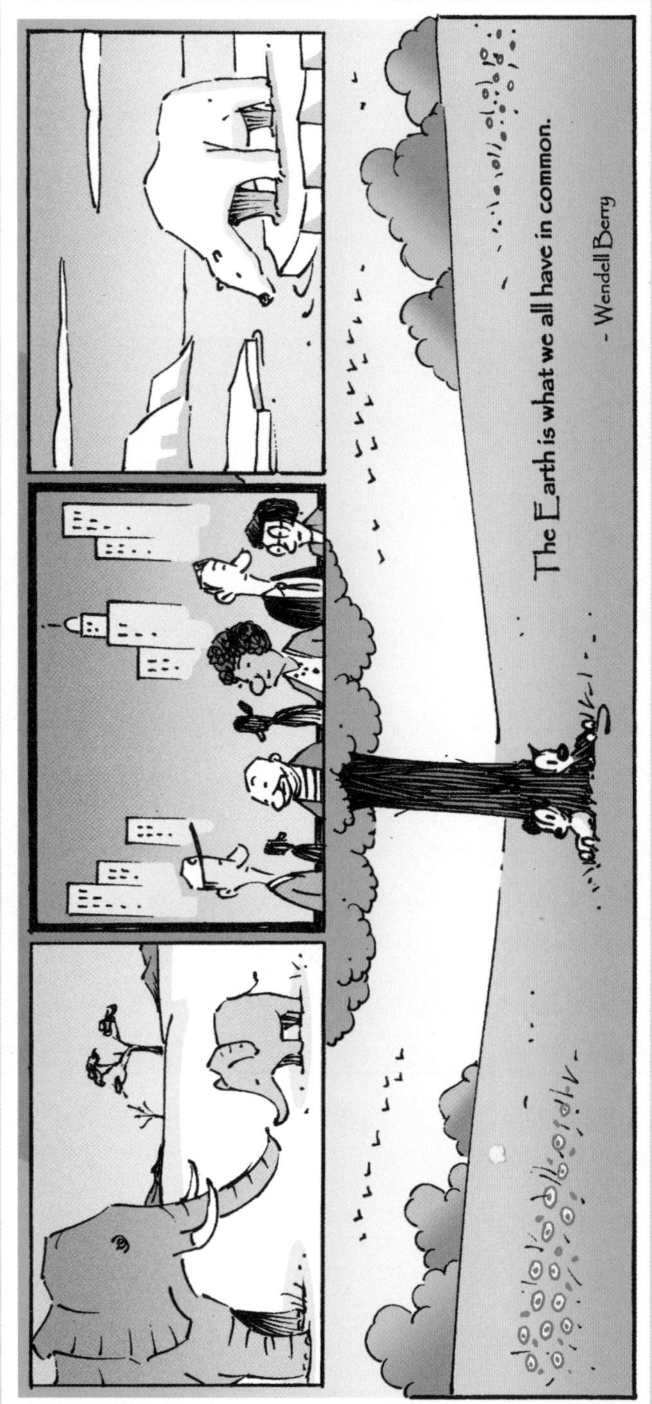
The Earth is what we all have in common.
- Wendell Berry

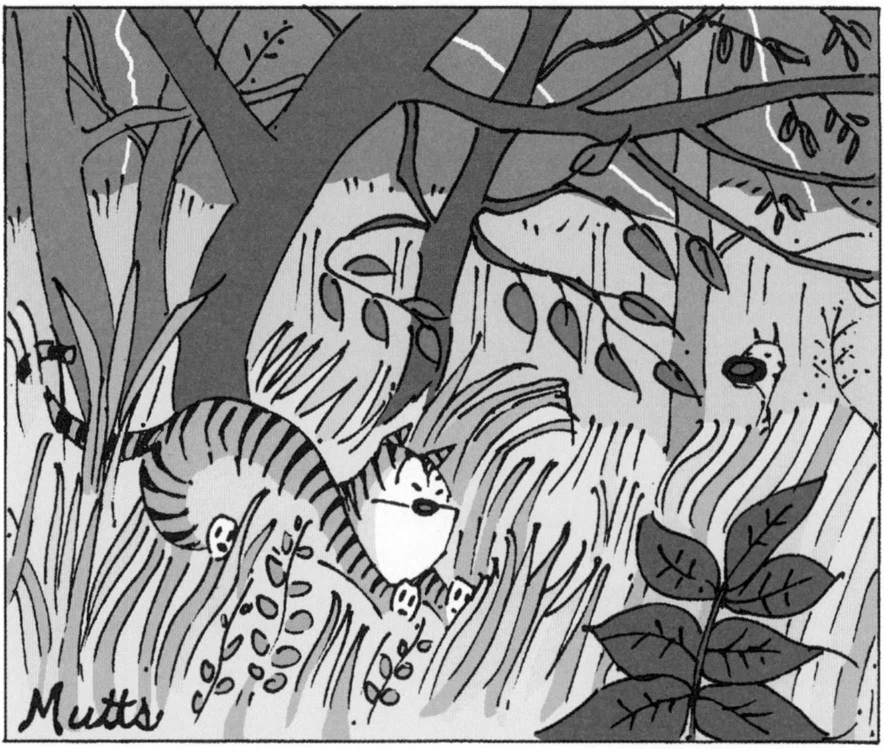
Mutts

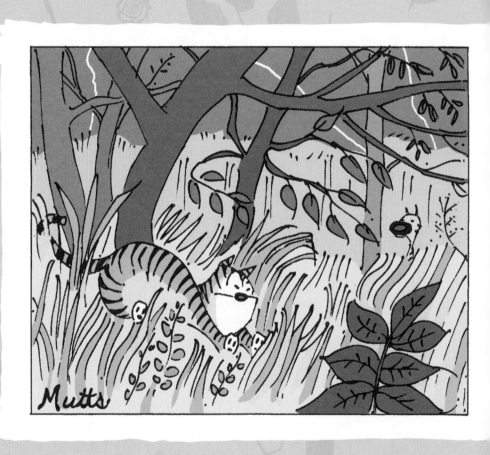

Keep It WILD

Nature supplies us with everything we need to live on this planet, starting with air, water, and the land under our feet. Nature needs space and to be left alone to keep regenerating. Animals need wild space to survive.

Sadly, nearly 38 percent of all known species on a global scale are on the verge of extinction. Since the 1960s, nearly half of the world's rainforests have been lost—and half of the world's species live in tropical rainforests. Our oceans are being depleted by overfishing. We must relearn to share our planet with the other almost nine million species. Diversity makes us whole.

How can we help? We can do a lot by giving nature space to keep it wild. Learning to appreciate nature is a great start. You can learn about the world's many different animals, birds, fish, plants, and ecosystems. And you can help in your own backyard and community. Create a safe habitat for wildlife and native plants near your home. If you have bats in your community, consider yourself lucky. Be thankful for bees; they are critical to our food supply.

Little things can make a big difference when everyone pitches in. Start a club to find places in your town to rewild or to plant native trees. Write letters to your local newspaper and speak up for animals and the planet.

We don't own the planet Earth, we belong to it. And we must share it with our wildlife.

—Steve Irwin

How to Keep It Wild

- Be a friend to all animals and nature.

- Learn about animals and their habitats so you can find out how to help them.

- If you have a yard, leave part of it wild for insects and critters.

- Put out bird feeders, birdbaths, and birdhouses.

- Plant a native garden for birds, bats, and other wildlife.

- Create a bee-friendly garden by planting flowers like daisies and marigolds.

- Plant milkweed for the monarch butterfly.

- Become active in your community.

- Speak up for animals and the earth.

- Start a club at school to help wildlife in your area.

TAP
TAP
TAP
TAP
TAP

I THINK YOU NEED TO RE-FILL THE BIRD FEEDER.

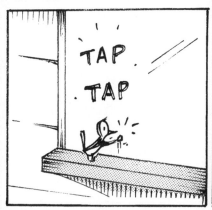

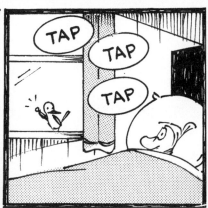

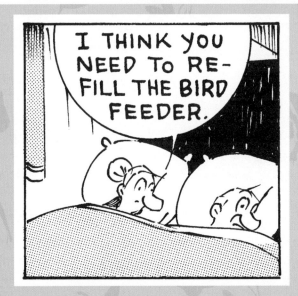

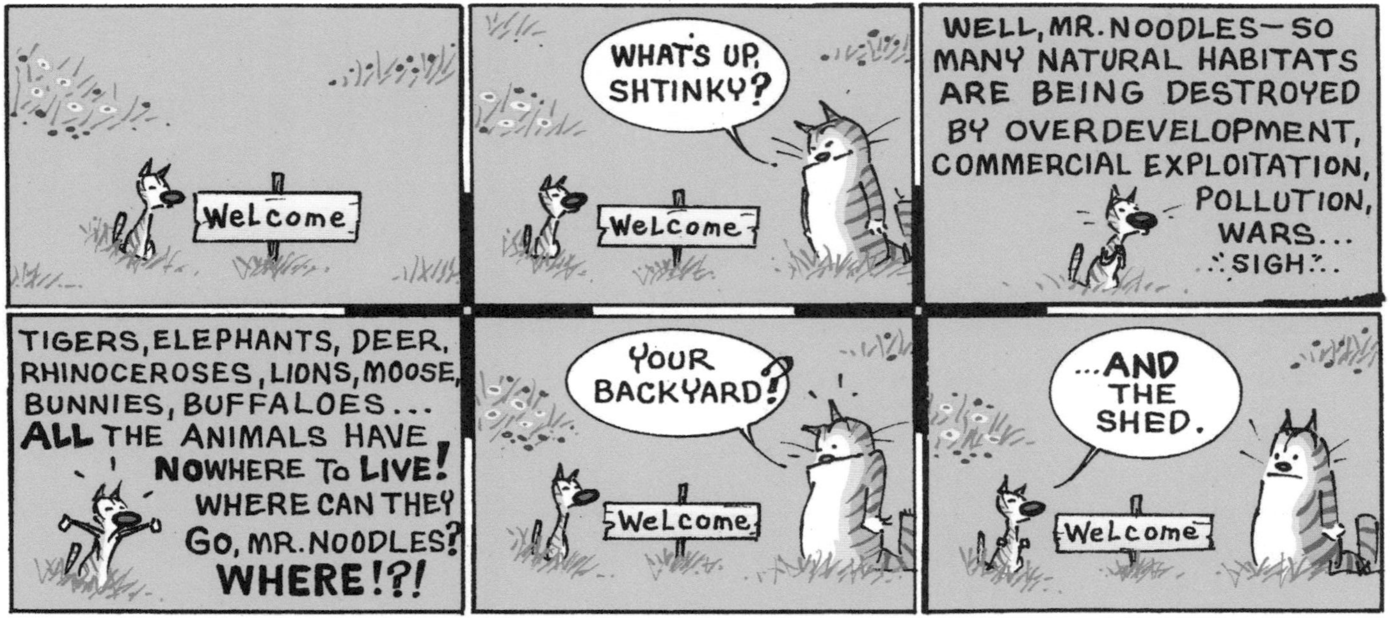
Welcome
WHAT'S UP, SHTINKY?
Welcome
WELL, MR. NOODLES—SO MANY NATURAL HABITATS ARE BEING DESTROYED BY OVERDEVELOPMENT, COMMERCIAL EXPLOITATION, POLLUTION, WARS... SIGH..
TIGERS, ELEPHANTS, DEER, RHINOCEROSES, LIONS, MOOSE, BUNNIES, BUFFALOES... ALL THE ANIMALS HAVE NOWHERE TO LIVE! WHERE CAN THEY GO, MR. NOODLES? WHERE!?!
YOUR BACKYARD!?
Welcome
...AND THE SHED.
Welcome

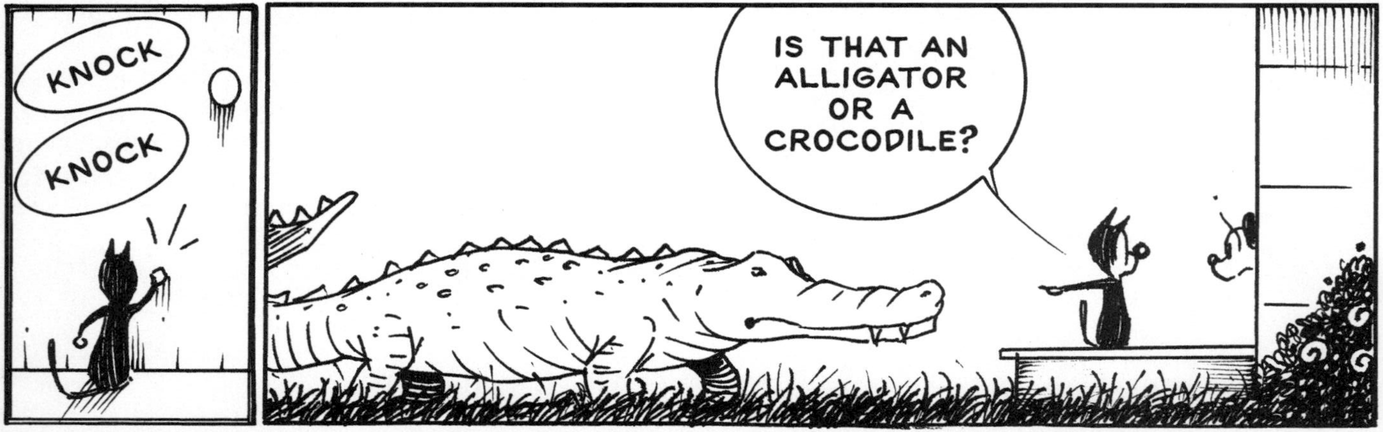
KNOCK
KNOCK
IS THAT AN ALLIGATOR OR A CROCODILE?

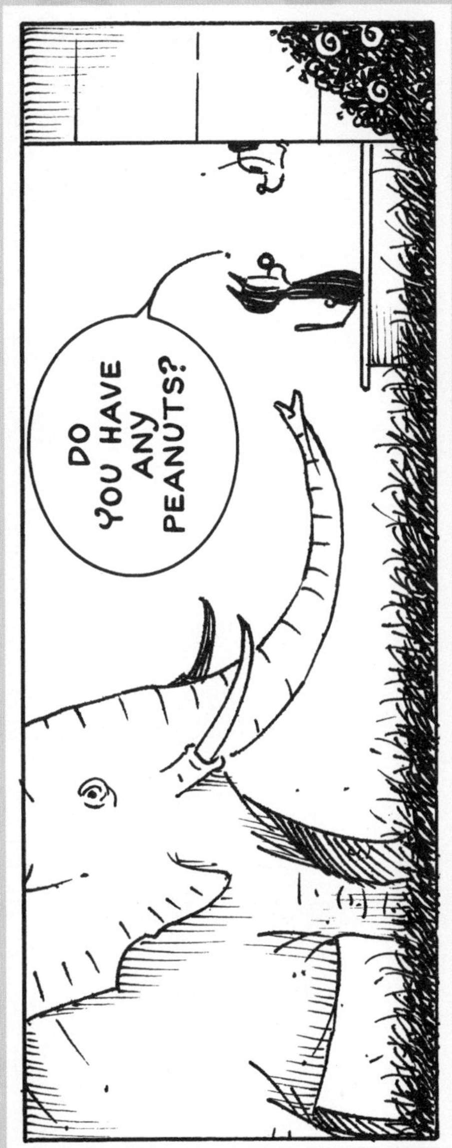
KNOCK
KNOCK
DO YOU HAVE ANY PEANUTS?

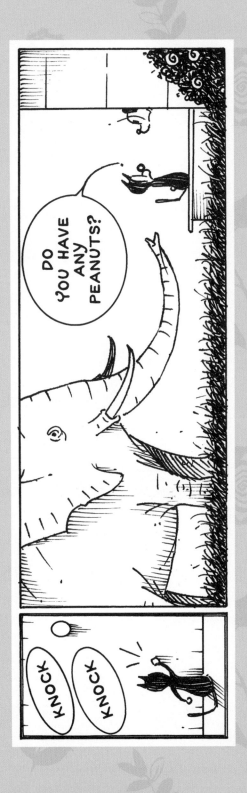

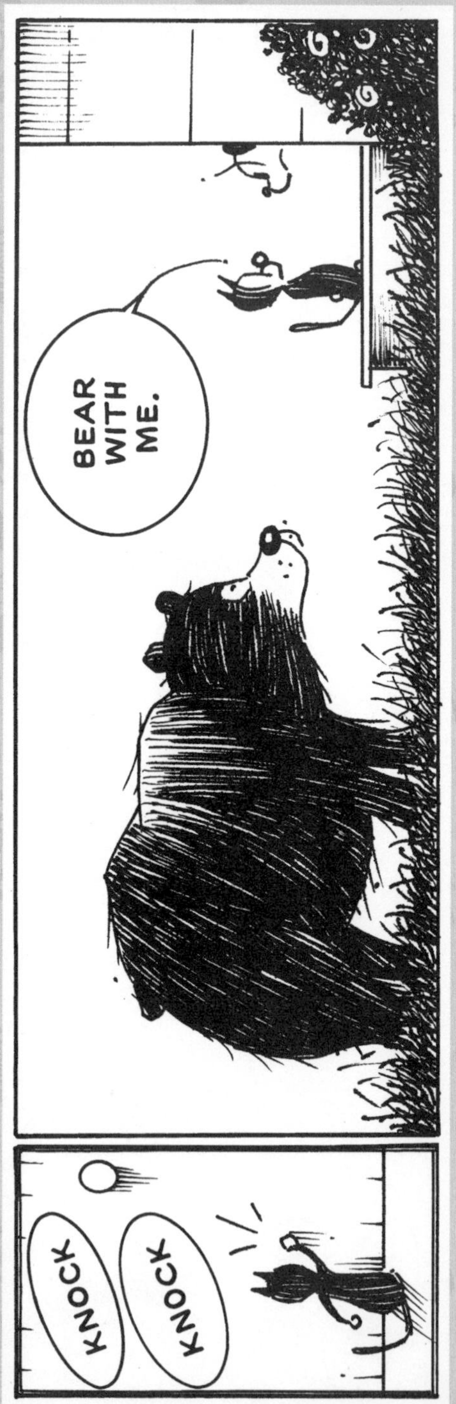
KNOCK
KNOCK
BEAR WITH ME.

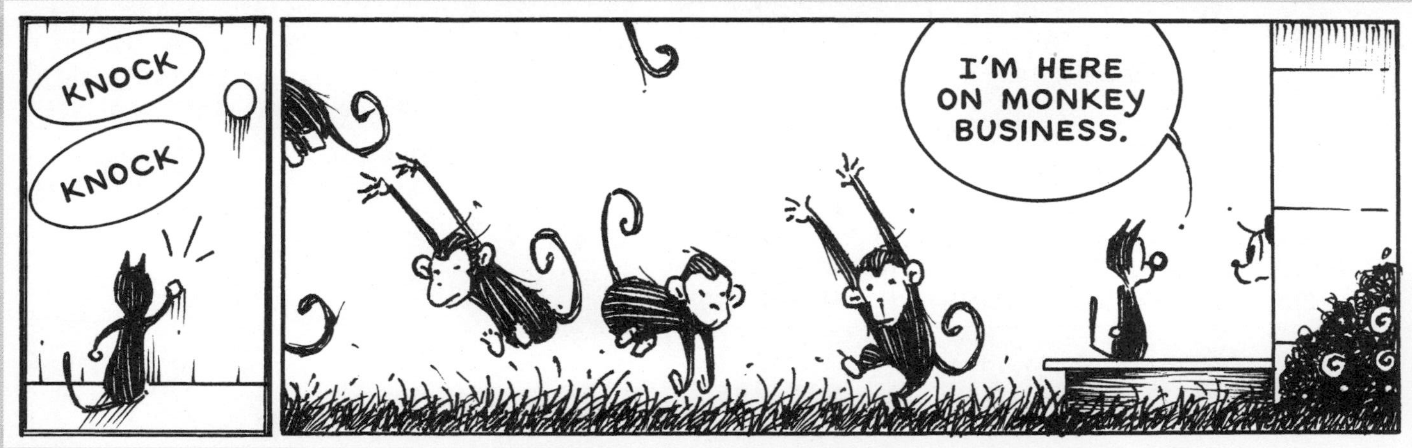
KNOCK
KNOCK
I'M HERE ON MONKEY BUSINESS.

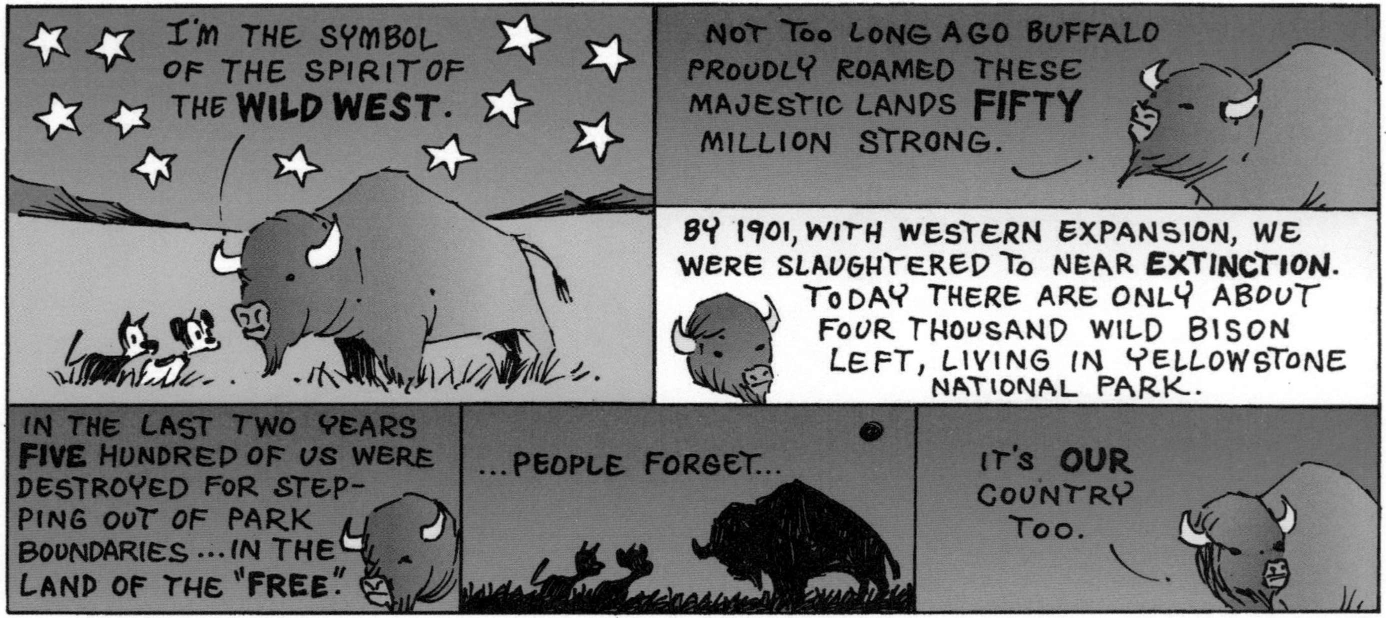
I'M THE SYMBOL OF THE SPIRIT OF THE WILD WEST.
NOT TOO LONG AGO BUFFALO PROUDLY ROAMED THESE MAJESTIC LANDS FIFTY MILLION STRONG.
BY 1901, WITH WESTERN EXPANSION, WE WERE SLAUGHTERED TO NEAR EXTINCTION. TODAY THERE ARE ONLY ABOUT FOUR THOUSAND WILD BISON LEFT, LIVING IN YELLOWSTONE NATIONAL PARK.
IN THE LAST TWO YEARS FIVE HUNDRED OF US WERE DESTROYED FOR STEP-PING OUT OF PARK BOUNDARIES... IN THE LAND OF THE "FREE".
...PEOPLE FORGET...
IT'S OUR COUNTRY TOO.

THIS LAND IS YOUR LAND,
THIS LAND IS MY LAND...

THIS LAND WAS MADE FOR YOU AND ME.

EARL, WHAT MAKES A TIGER "EN-DANGERED"?
IT'S WHEN A SPECIES IS "IN DANGER" OF BECOMING EXTINCT.
EXTINCT?!
GONE FOREVER.

HOLD ME.

I'VE GOT TO SAVE THE ENDANGERED TIGERS!
HOW?
I WAS THINKING OF SENDING 'EM ALL MY TREATS

WHY? WHY? WHY?
WHY ARE THERE ALL THESE ENDANGERED ANIMALS!?!
I GUESS THIS OL' PLANET IS JUST NOT BIG ENOUGH ANYMORE

ARE YOU KIDDIN' ME!?!

EARL, MOOCH, I'VE DECIDED TO **SAVE** THE WORLD'S TIGERS.
YOU!?!

SOME-BODY HAS TO.

I WILL SAVE THE TIGERS
I WILL SAVE THE TIGERS.
I WILL SAVE THE TIGERS.
I WILL
I'M A BIG BELIEVER IN POSITIVE THINKING

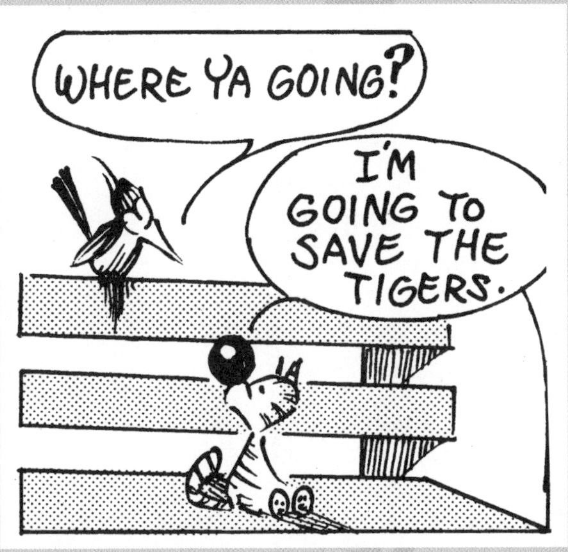
WHERE YA GOING?
I'M GOING TO SAVE THE TIGERS.

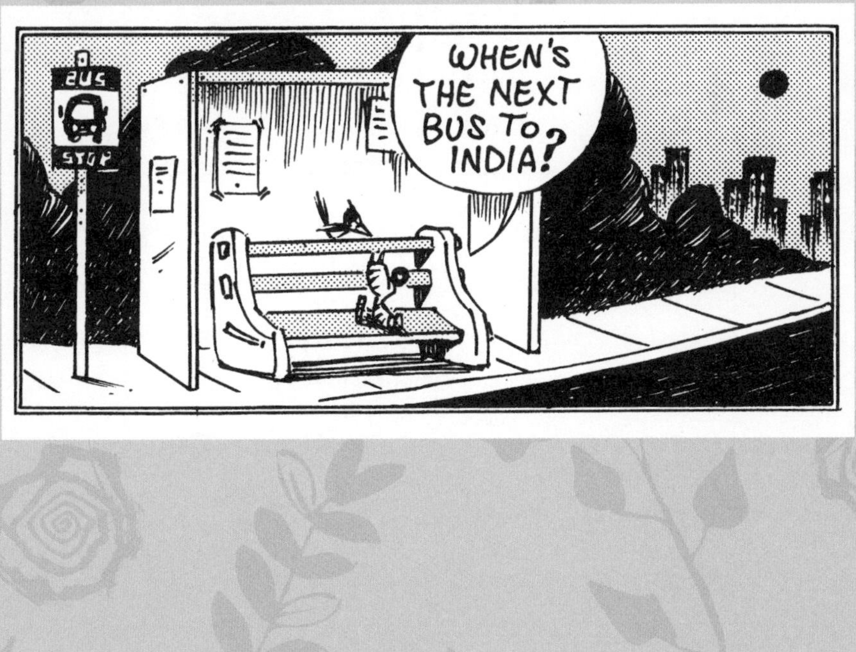
BUS
STOP
WHEN'S THE NEXT BUS TO INDIA?

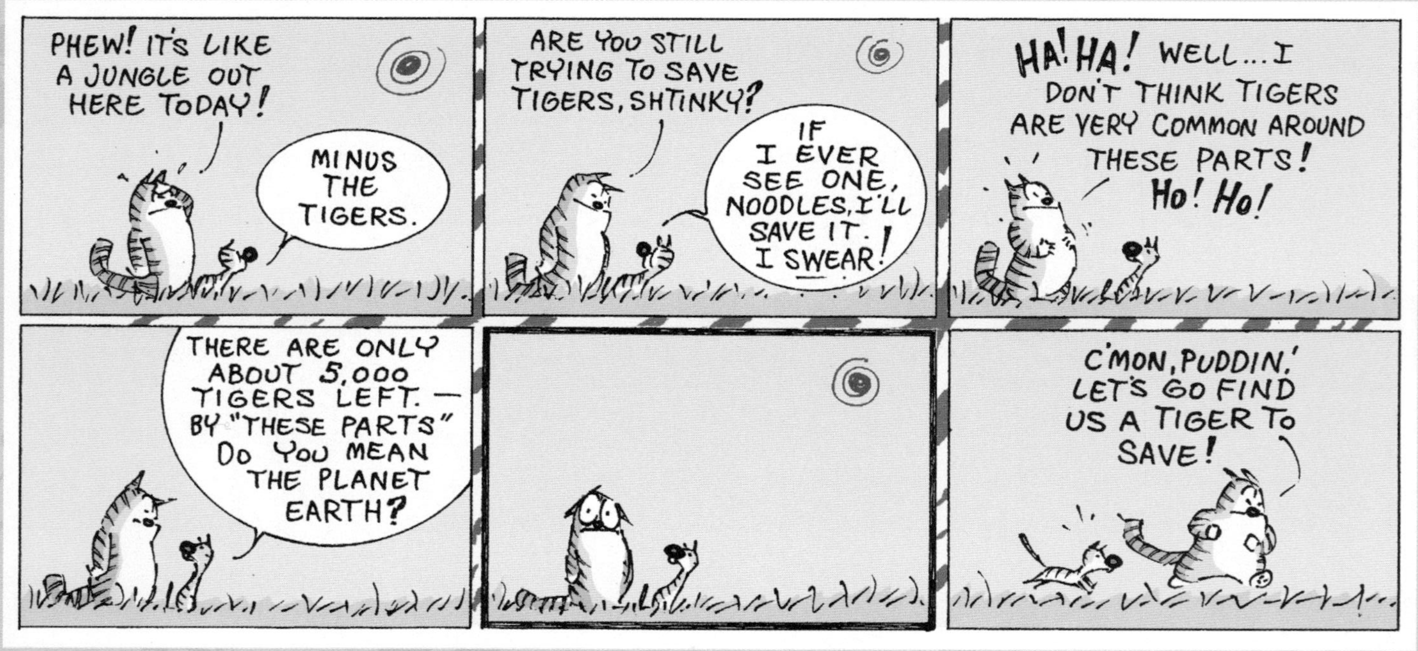

PHEW! IT'S LIKE A JUNGLE OUT HERE TODAY!
MINUS THE TIGERS.
ARE YOU STILL TRYING TO SAVE TIGERS, SHTINKY?
IF I EVER SEE ONE, NOODLES, I'LL SAVE IT. I SWEAR!
HA! HA! WELL... I DON'T THINK TIGERS ARE VERY COMMON AROUND THESE PARTS!
HO! HO!
THERE ARE ONLY ABOUT 5,000 TIGERS LEFT. — BY "THESE PARTS" DO YOU MEAN THE PLANET EARTH?
C'MON, PUDDIN,' LET'S GO FIND US A TIGER TO SAVE!

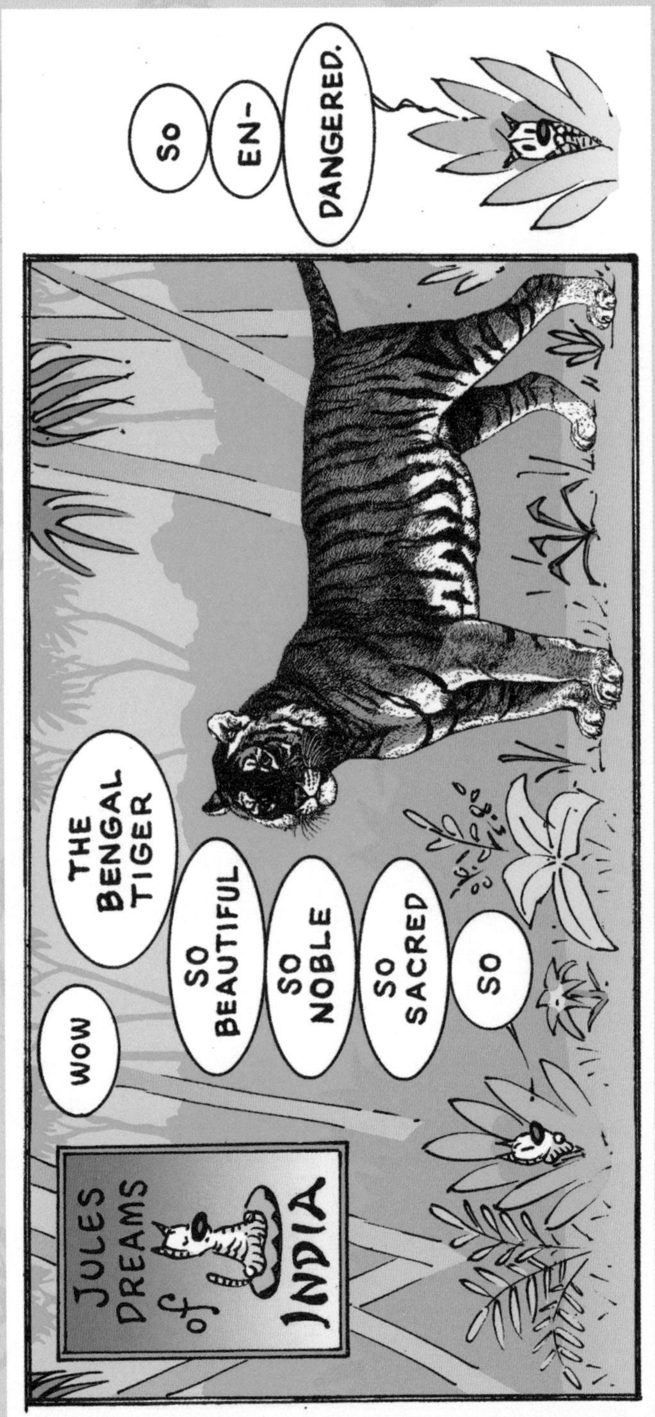
JULES DREAMS of INDIA
WOW
THE BENGAL TIGER
SO BEAUTIFUL
SO NOBLE
SO SACRED
SO
So
EN-
DANGERED.

JULES DREAMS of INDIA
NAMASTE

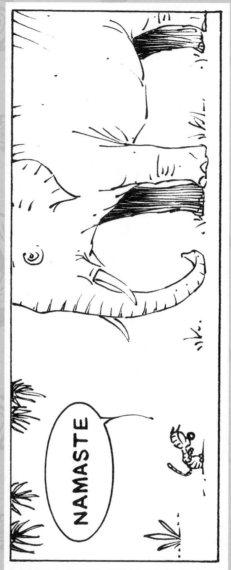

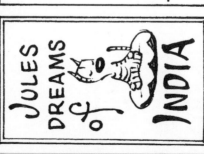

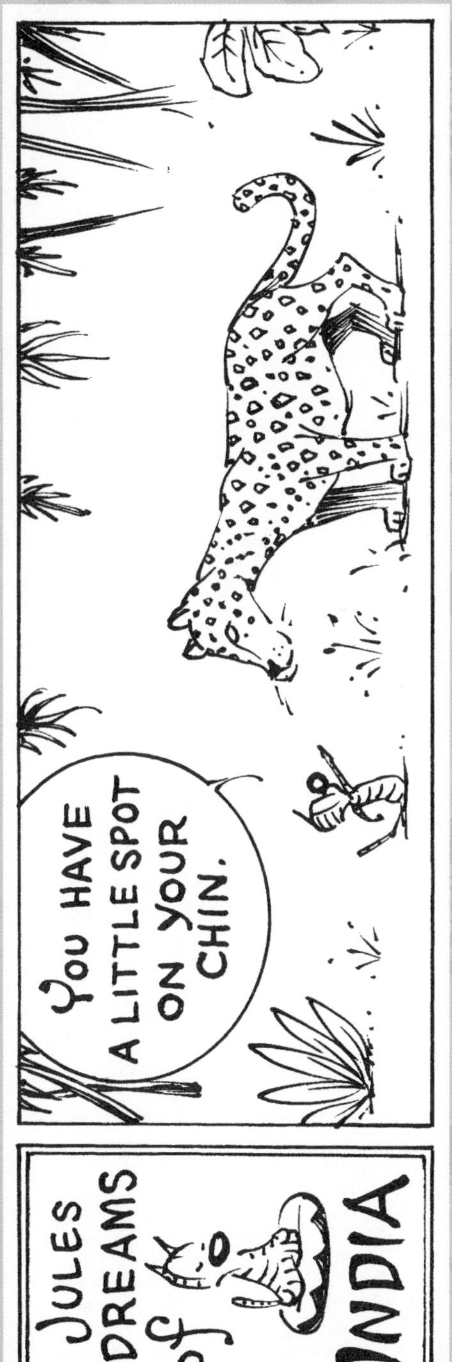
JULES DREAMS of INDIA
YOU HAVE A LITTLE SPOT ON YOUR CHIN.

JULES DREAMS of INDIA
ANY REQUESTS ?

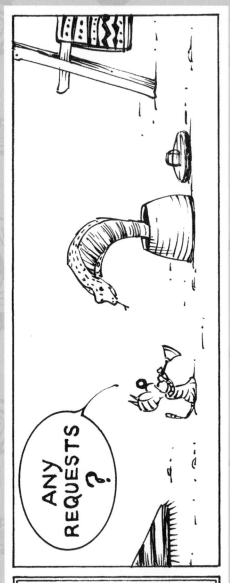

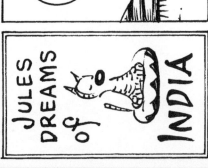

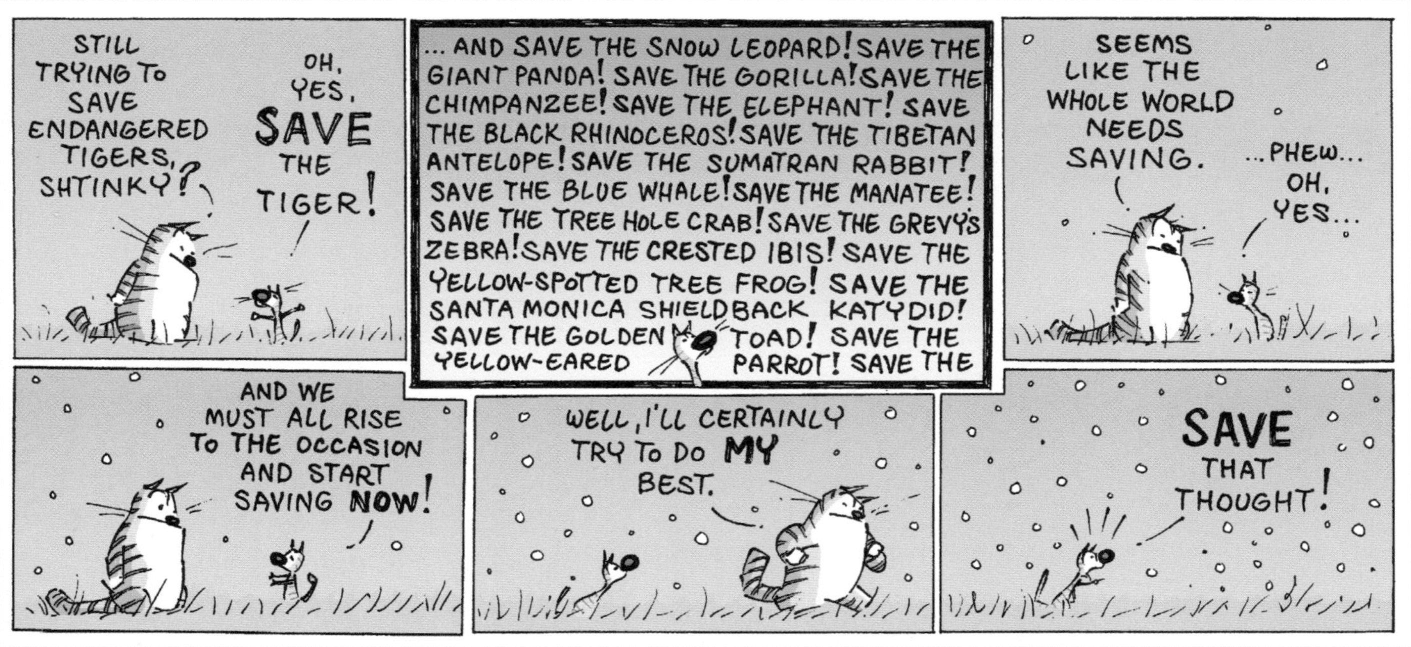
STILL TRYING TO SAVE ENDANGERED TIGERS, SHTINKY?
OH, YES. SAVE THE TIGER!
... AND SAVE THE SNOW LEOPARD! SAVE THE GIANT PANDA! SAVE THE GORILLA! SAVE THE CHIMPANZEE! SAVE THE ELEPHANT! SAVE THE BLACK RHINOCEROS! SAVE THE TIBETAN ANTELOPE! SAVE THE SUMATRAN RABBIT! SAVE THE BLUE WHALE! SAVE THE MANATEE! SAVE THE TREE HOLE CRAB! SAVE THE GREVY'S ZEBRA! SAVE THE CRESTED IBIS! SAVE THE YELLOW-SPOTTED TREE FROG! SAVE THE SANTA MONICA SHIELDBACK KATYDID! SAVE THE GOLDEN TOAD! SAVE THE YELLOW-EARED PARROT! SAVE THE
SEEMS LIKE THE WHOLE WORLD NEEDS SAVING.
...PHEW... OH, YES...
AND WE MUST ALL RISE TO THE OCCASION AND START SAVING NOW!
WELL, I'LL CERTAINLY TRY TO DO MY BEST.
SAVE THAT THOUGHT!

WHALE WATCH
WILL I DO?

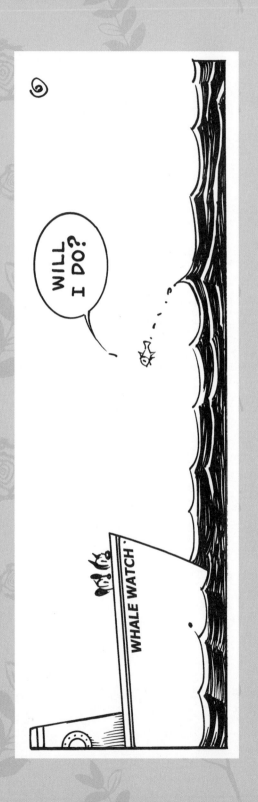

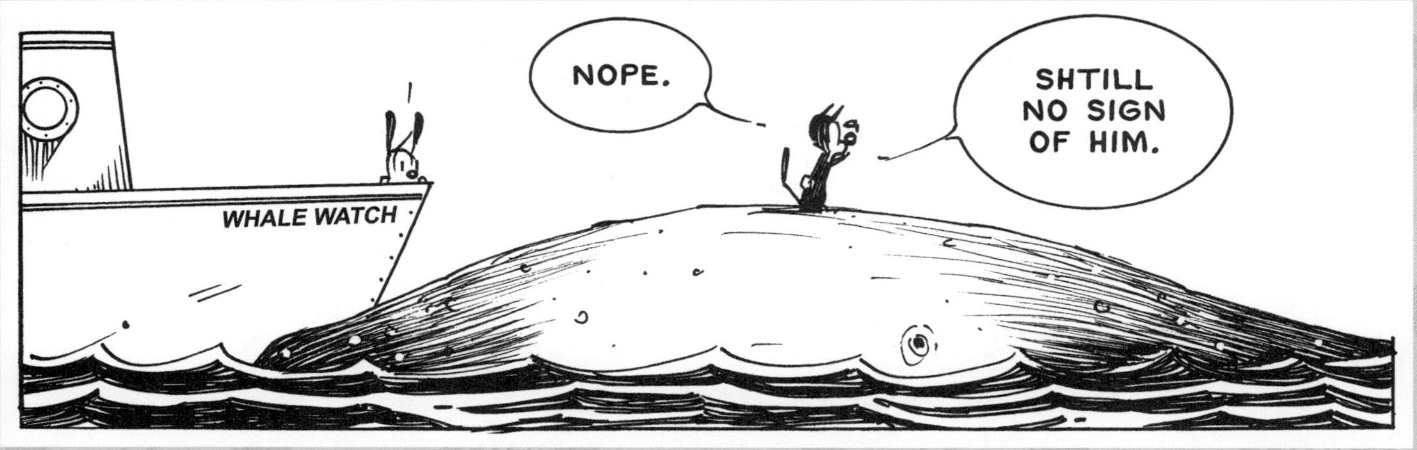
WHALE WATCH
NOPE.
SHTILL NO SIGN OF HIM.

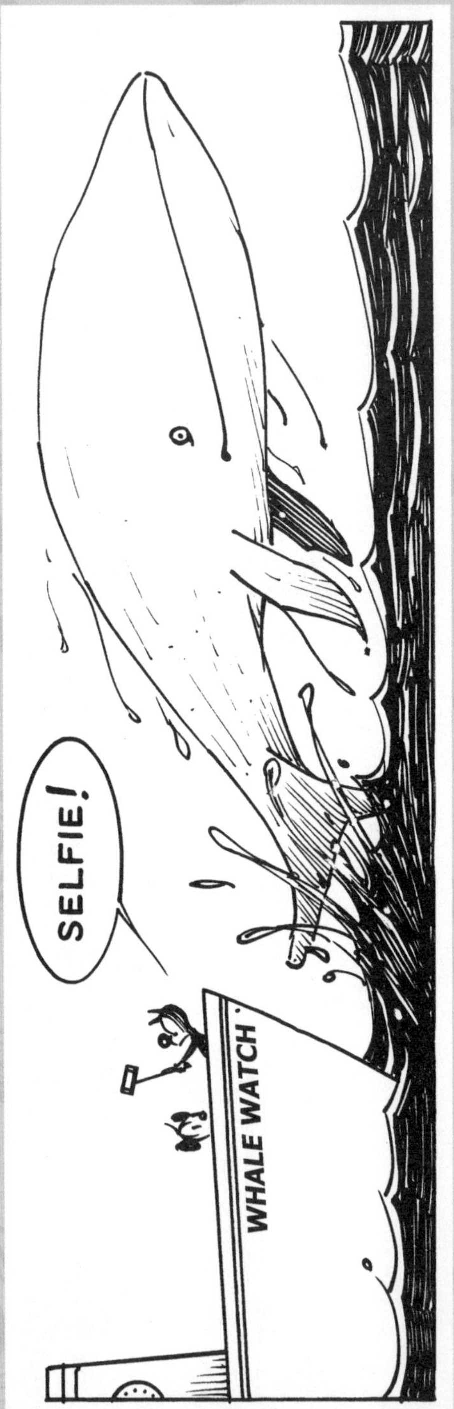
SELFIE!
WHALE WATCH

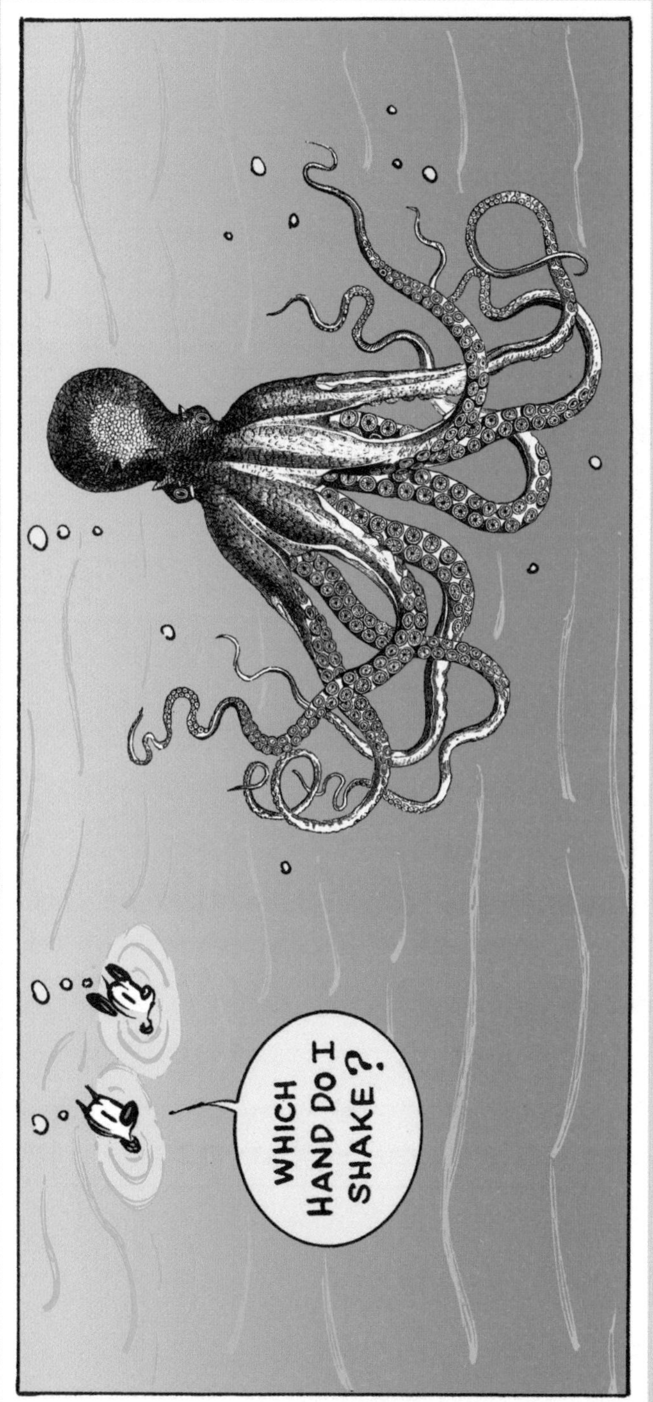
WHICH HAND DO I SHAKE?

NARWHALS ARE LIKE UNICORNS BUT...
EVEN MORE MAGICAL.
HOW'S THAT?
THEY'RE REAL.

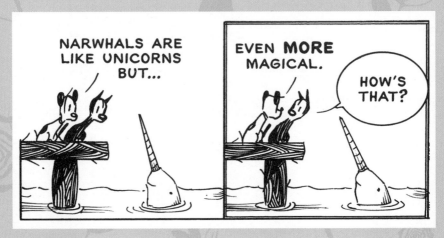

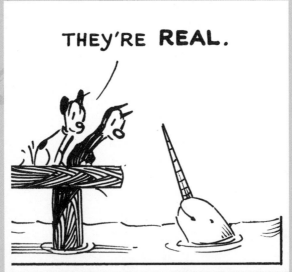

I'M TELLING YOU— SOME SCIENTISTS BELIEVE LOBSTERS DON'T HAVE FEEL- INGS.
WELL,
BASED ON THAT RESEARCH ...

LOBSTERS BELIEVE SOME SCIENTISTS DON'T HAVE FEELINGS!

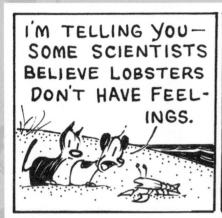

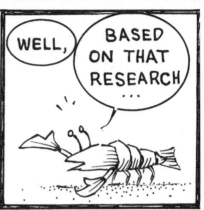

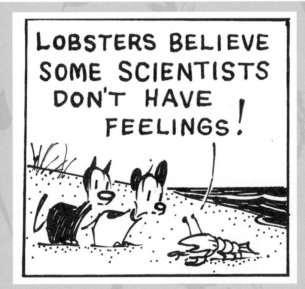

SCIENTISTS HAVE CONCLUDED THAT FISH CAN FEEL PAIN
YET HUMANS STILL OVERFISH AND POLLUTE THE OCEAN
NOW
THAT HURTS

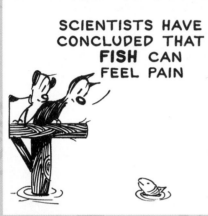

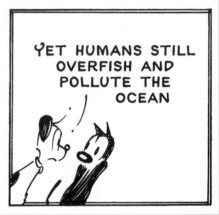

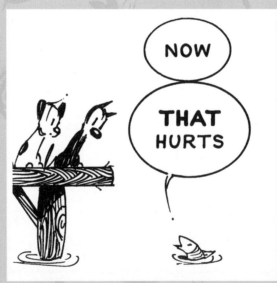

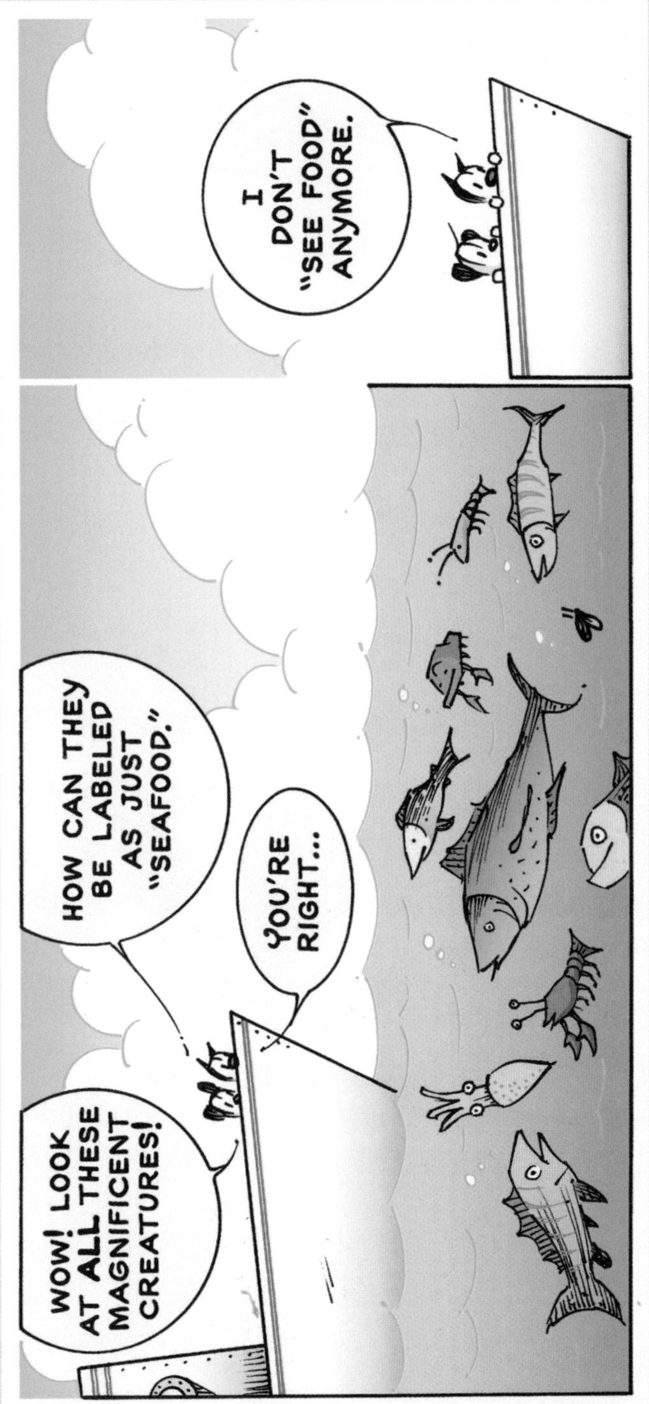
WOW! LOOK AT ALL THESE MAGNIFICENT CREATURES!
HOW CAN THEY BE LABELED AS JUST "SEAFOOD."
YOU'RE RIGHT...
I DON'T "SEE FOOD" ANYMORE.

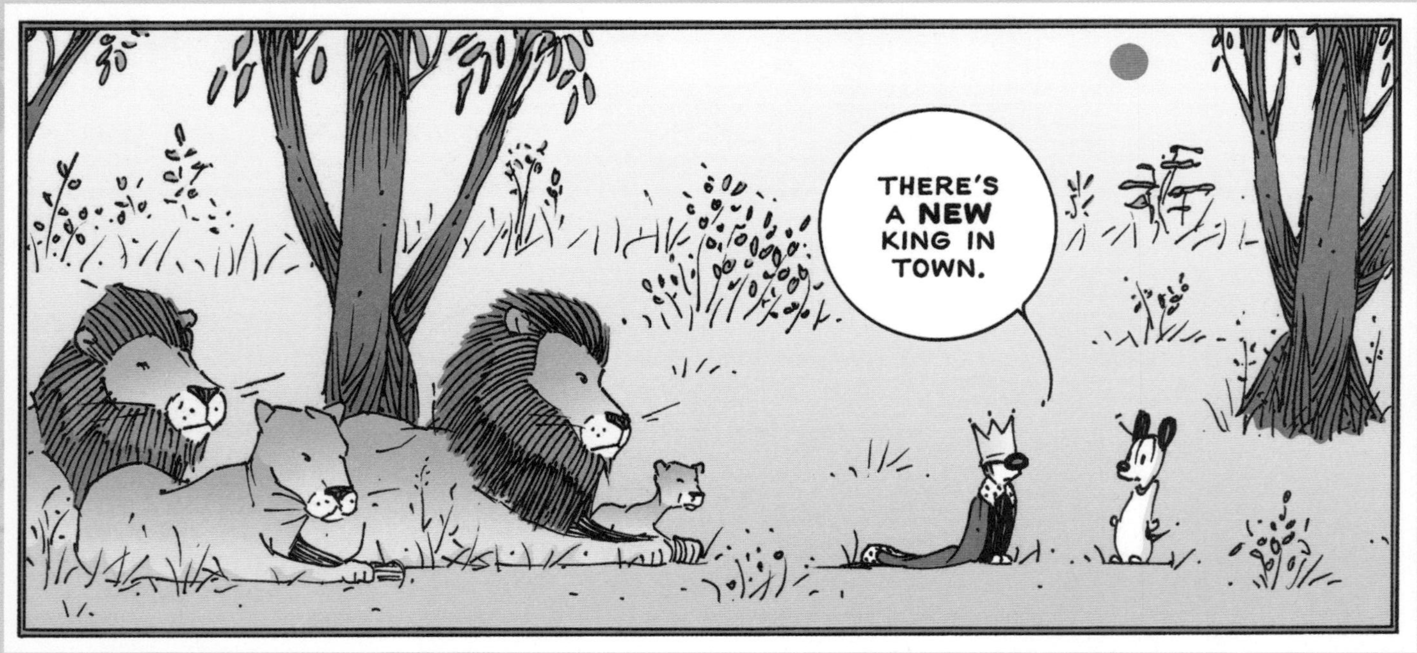
THERE'S A NEW KING IN TOWN.

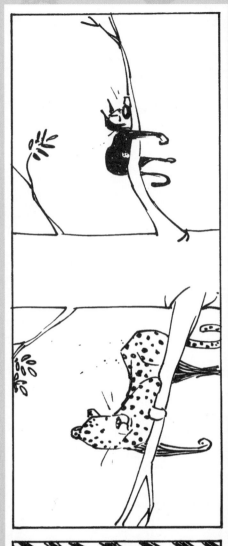

MOOCH DREAMS of AFRICA

117

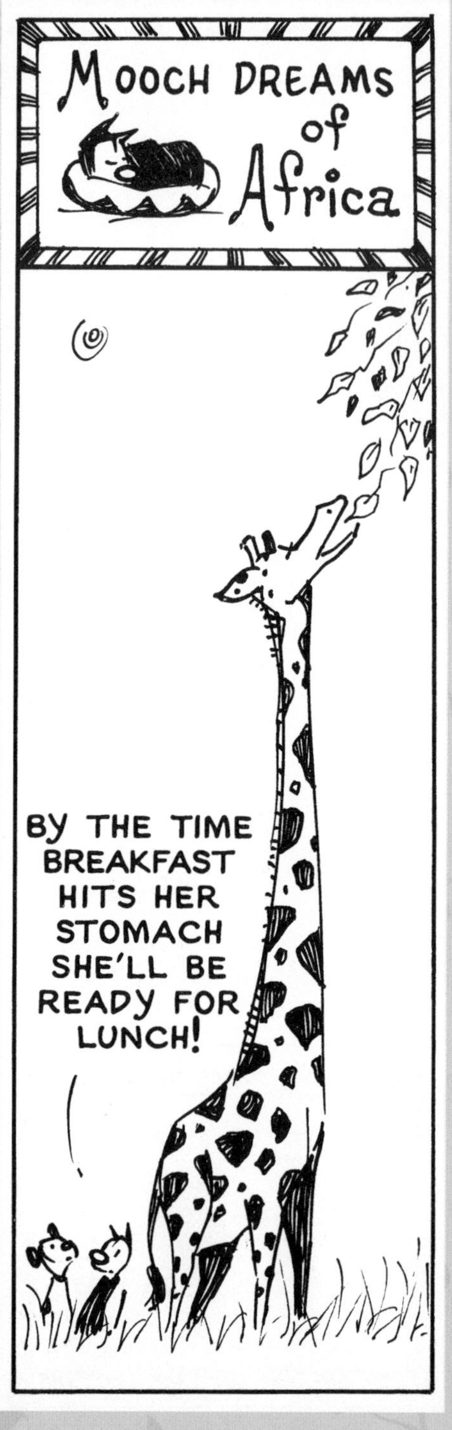
MOOCH DREAMS of Africa
BY THE TIME BREAKFAST HITS HER STOMACH SHE'LL BE READY FOR LUNCH!

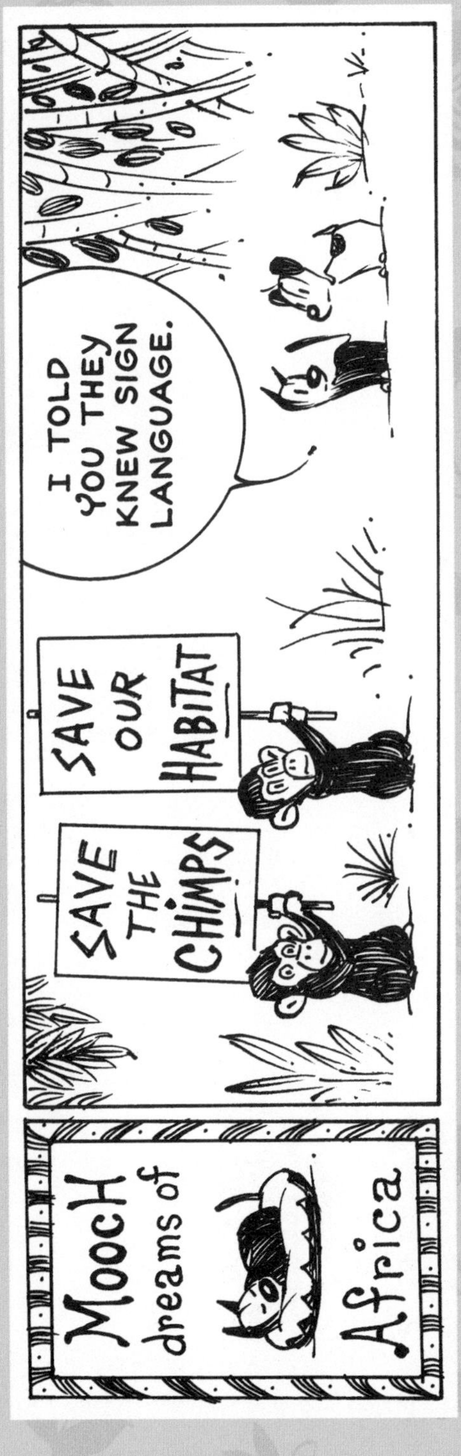
Mooch dreams of Africa
SAVE THE CHIMPS
SAVE OUR HABITAT
I TOLD YOU THEY KNEW SIGN LANGUAGE.

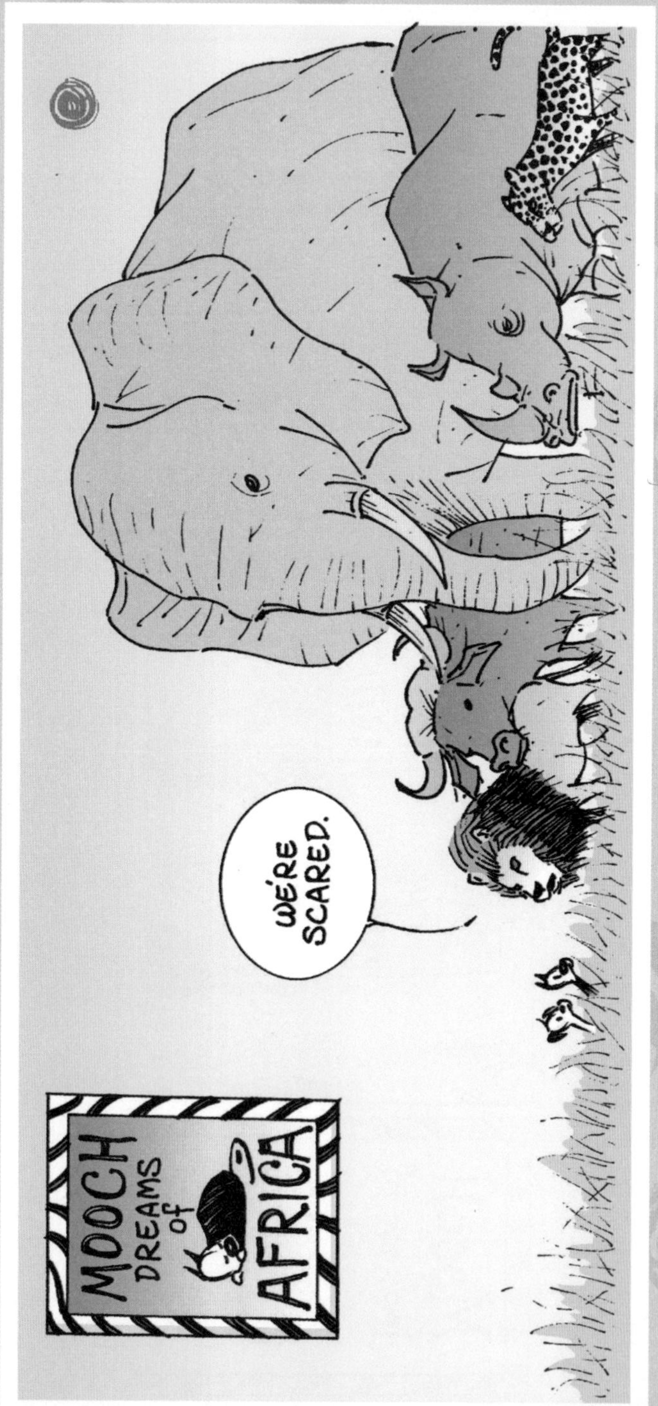
MOOCH DREAMS of AFRICA
WE'RE SCARED.

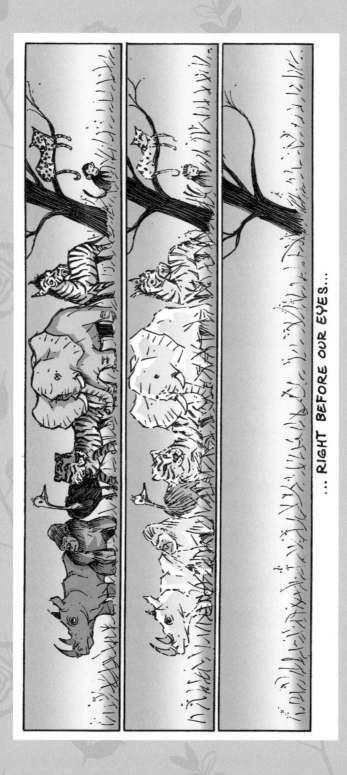

... RIGHT BEFORE OUR EYES...

121

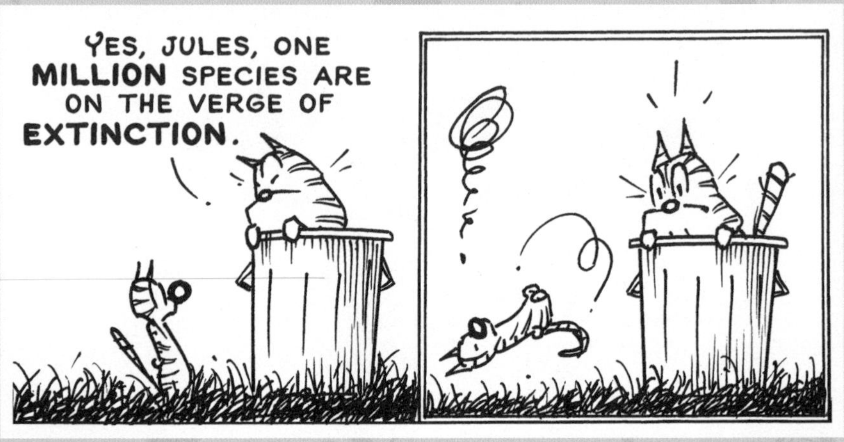
YES, JULES, ONE MILLION SPECIES ARE ON THE VERGE OF EXTINCTION.

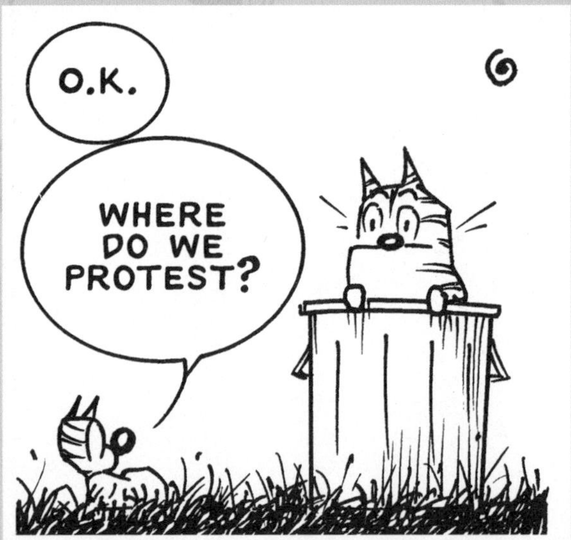
O.K.
WHERE DO WE PROTEST?

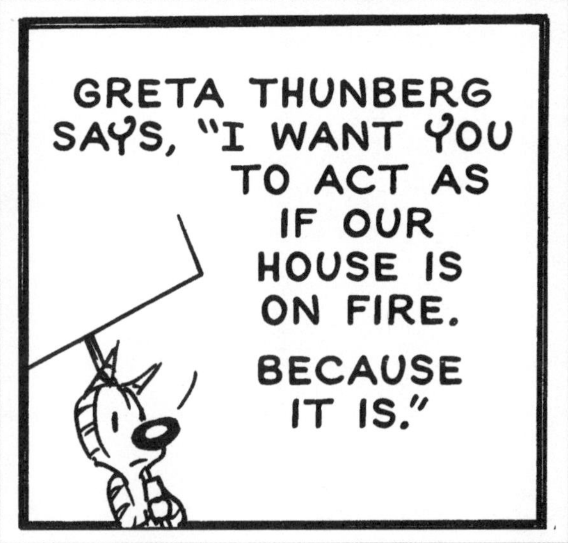
GRETA THUNBERG SAYS, "I WANT YOU TO ACT AS IF OUR HOUSE IS ON FIRE.
BECAUSE IT IS."

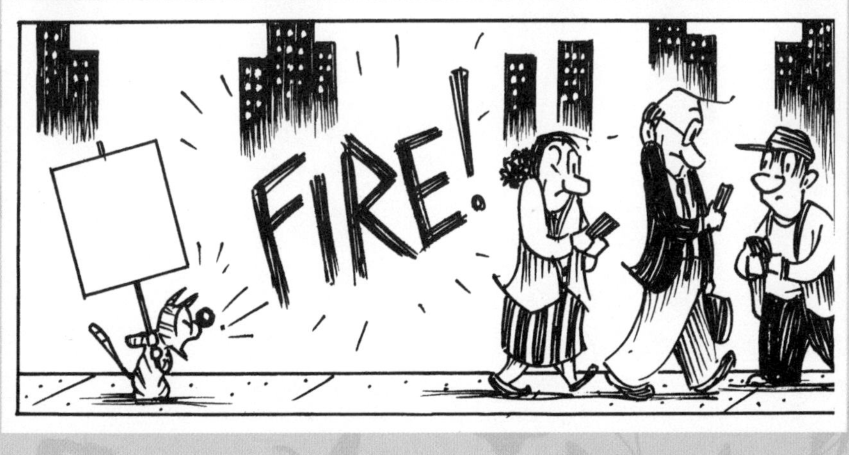
FIRE!

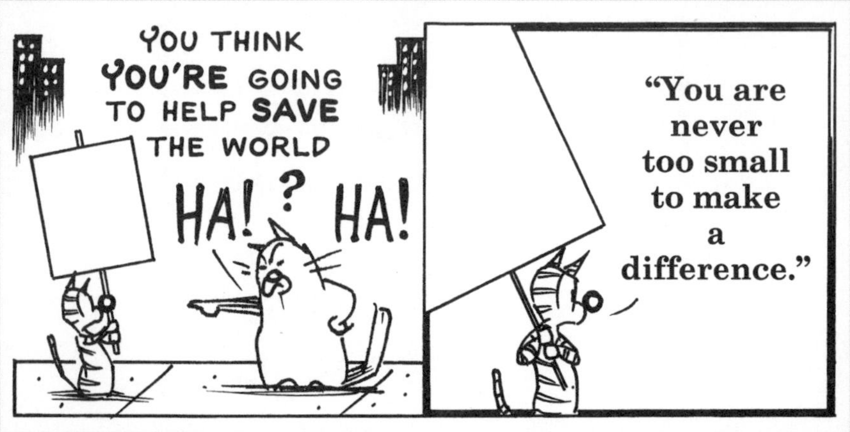
YOU THINK YOU'RE GOING TO HELP SAVE THE WORLD
HA! ? HA!
"You are never too small to make a difference."

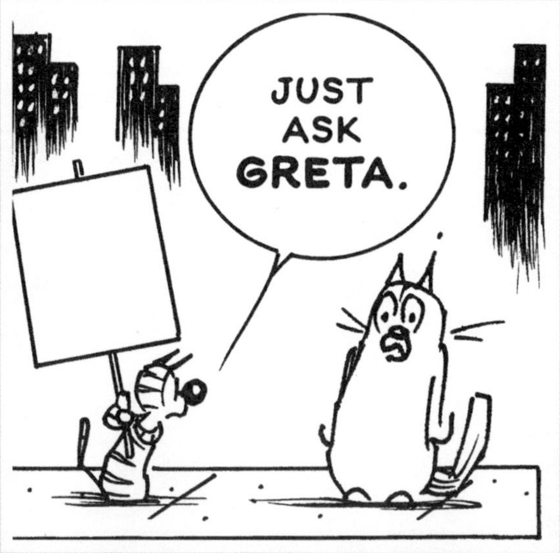
JUST ASK GRETA.

*O*nly if we understand, will we care.
Only if we care, will we help.
Only if we help, shall all be saved.

~ Jane Goodall

Because all creatures are connected, each must be cherished with love and respect, for all of us as living creatures are dependent on one another.

~ Pope Francis

PEACE TO ALL BEINGS

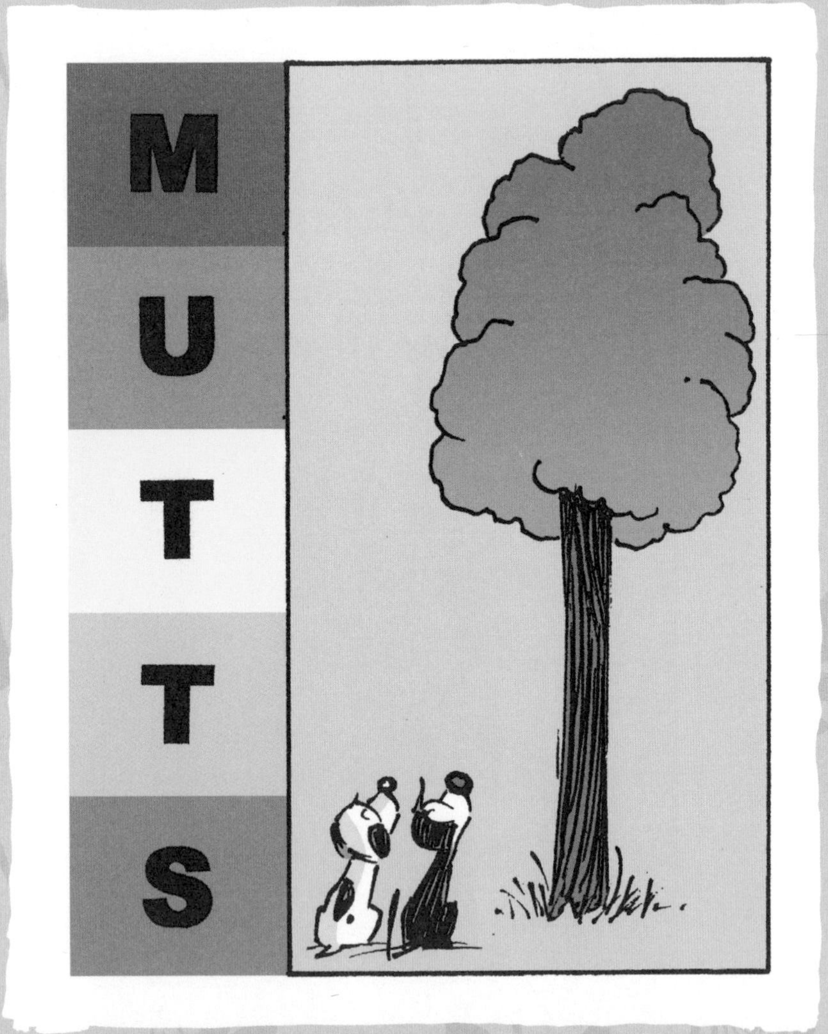
MUTTS

Keep It GREEN

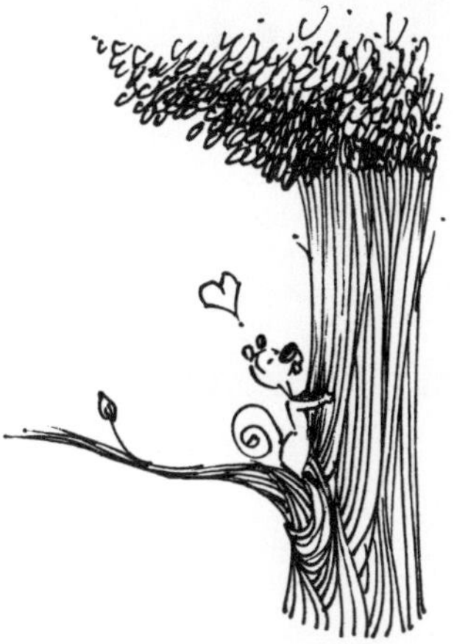

Keeping the earth clean and wild will go a long way toward keeping it green. Trees are the longest-living organisms on the planet, with some living thousands of years. Trees and plants provide the oxygen needed for all life, provide habitats for birds and many other animals, and offer shade to keep us cool. Encouraging people in your town to plant more trees (and to save existing ones) can help a lot. All species call Earth their home. They, and we, deserve the habitats and climate required to thrive.

Since farming animals for food requires a lot of land and water (and causes pollution), we can help keep the earth green by eating less meat and more plants. Reducing or eliminating our dependency on fossil fuels and moving to cleaner energy sources such as the sun and wind will help enormously as well.

These choices will also help to combat climate change. Each of us can do our part to make personal changes and to raise awareness. Keeping it kind will help convince others to join you. You are powerful and part of the generation that will make the changes we need in this world on a grand scale.

Unless someone like you cares a whole awful lot, nothing is going to get better. It's not.

—Dr. Seuss, *The Lorax*

How to Keep It Green

- Connect with nature. Play outside!
- Plant native trees and plants. And then plant some more.
- Start a vegetable garden.
- Make "seed bombs."
- When possible, buy organic.

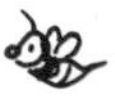

- Appreciate what others are doing to help. Write thank-you notes.
- Hold fundraisers to support green projects in your community.
- Get your school involved.
- Keep it fun!

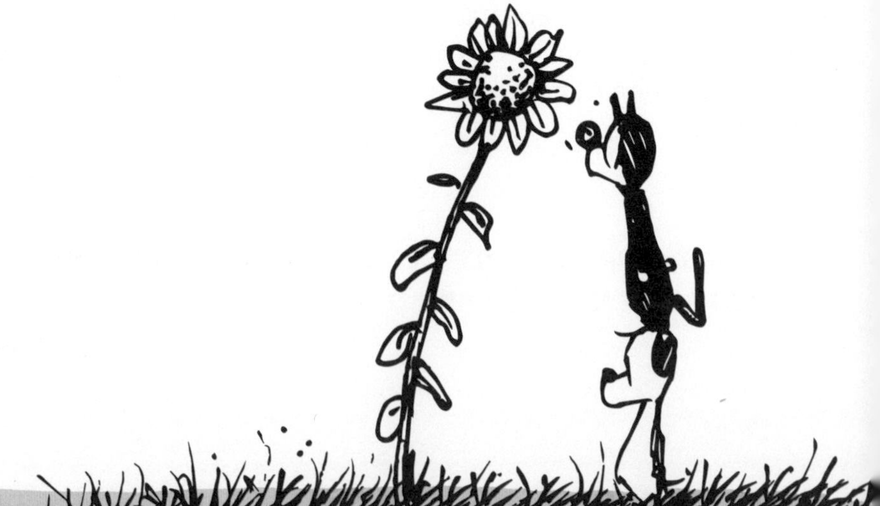

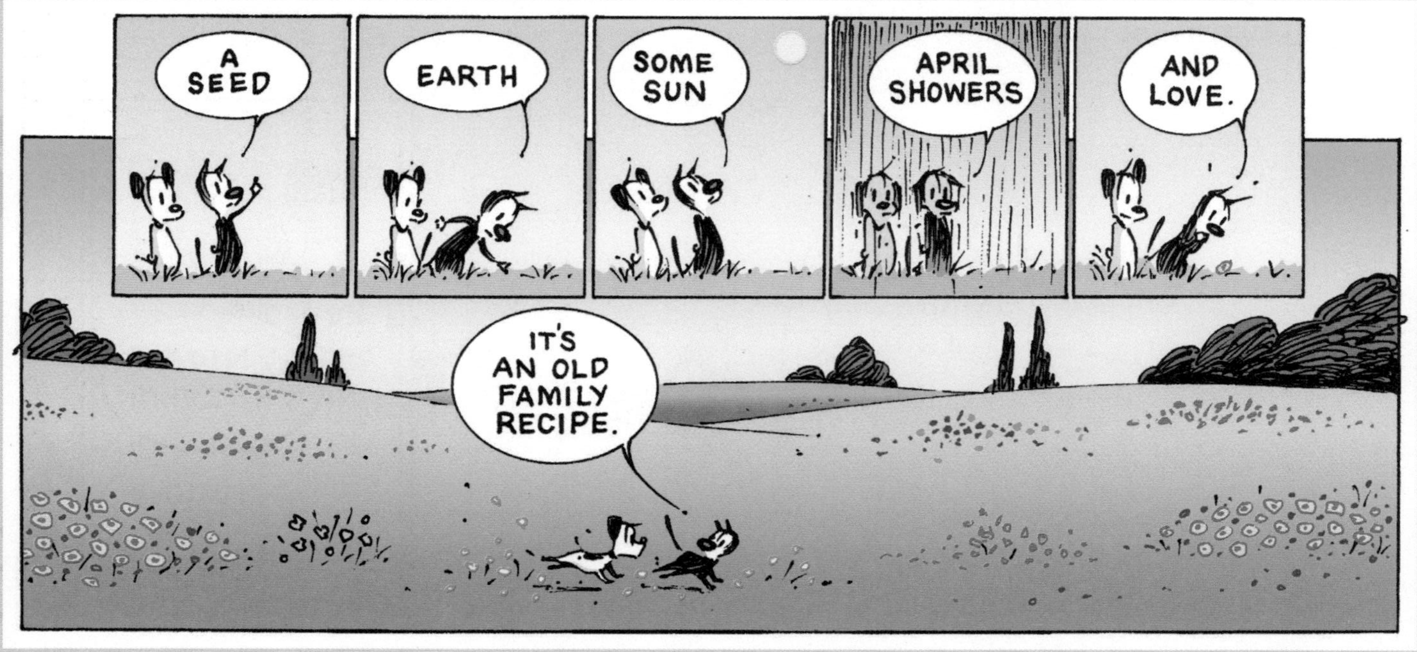
A SEED
EARTH
SOME SUN
APRIL SHOWERS
AND LOVE.
IT'S AN OLD FAMILY RECIPE.

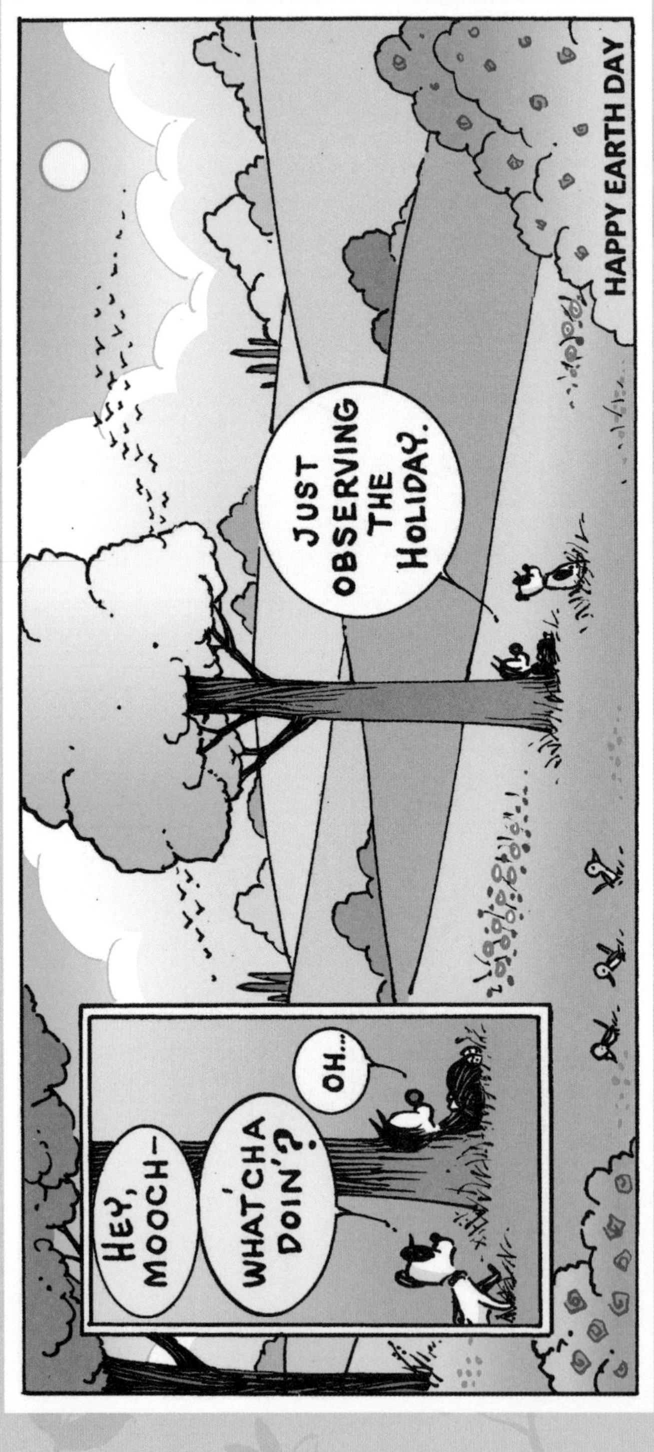
HEY, MOOCH—
WHATCHA DOIN'?
OH...
JUST OBSERVING THE HOLIDAY.
HAPPY EARTH DAY

JULES' EARTH DAY CELEBRATIONS
THE AMAZON RAIN FOREST

MOOCH! TOMORROW'S EARTH DAY!
YESH!
A TIME TO REMEMBER THE FRAGILITY OF OUR PRECIOUS PLANET AND TO COMMIT TO PROTECTING ITS BEAUTY AND WELL-BEING.
YESH!
I'LL BE WALKING ON MY TIPPY-TOES ALL DAY.

HAPPY EARTH DAY, EARL!
FOR ME?
I THOUGHT I'D PICK YOU UP A LITTLE SHOMETHING.
WHAT IS IT?
SHOME EARTH.

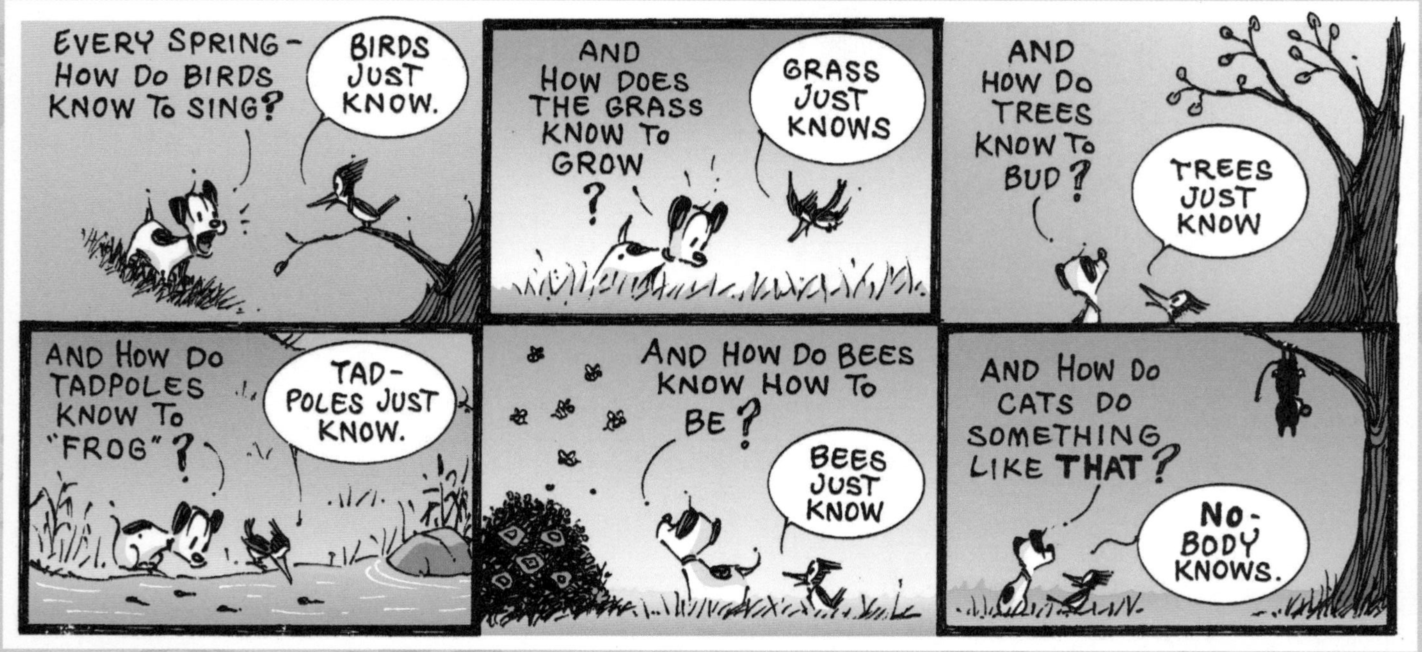
EVERY SPRING - HOW DO BIRDS KNOW TO SING?
BIRDS JUST KNOW.
AND HOW DOES THE GRASS KNOW TO GROW?
GRASS JUST KNOWS
AND HOW DO TREES KNOW TO BUD?
TREES JUST KNOW
AND HOW DO TADPOLES KNOW TO "FROG"?
TAD-POLES JUST KNOW.
AND HOW DO BEES KNOW HOW TO BE?
BEES JUST KNOW
AND HOW DO CATS DO SOMETHING LIKE THAT?
NO-BODY KNOWS.

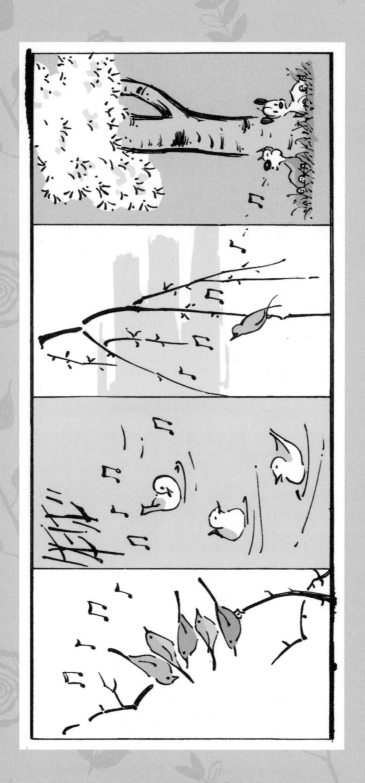

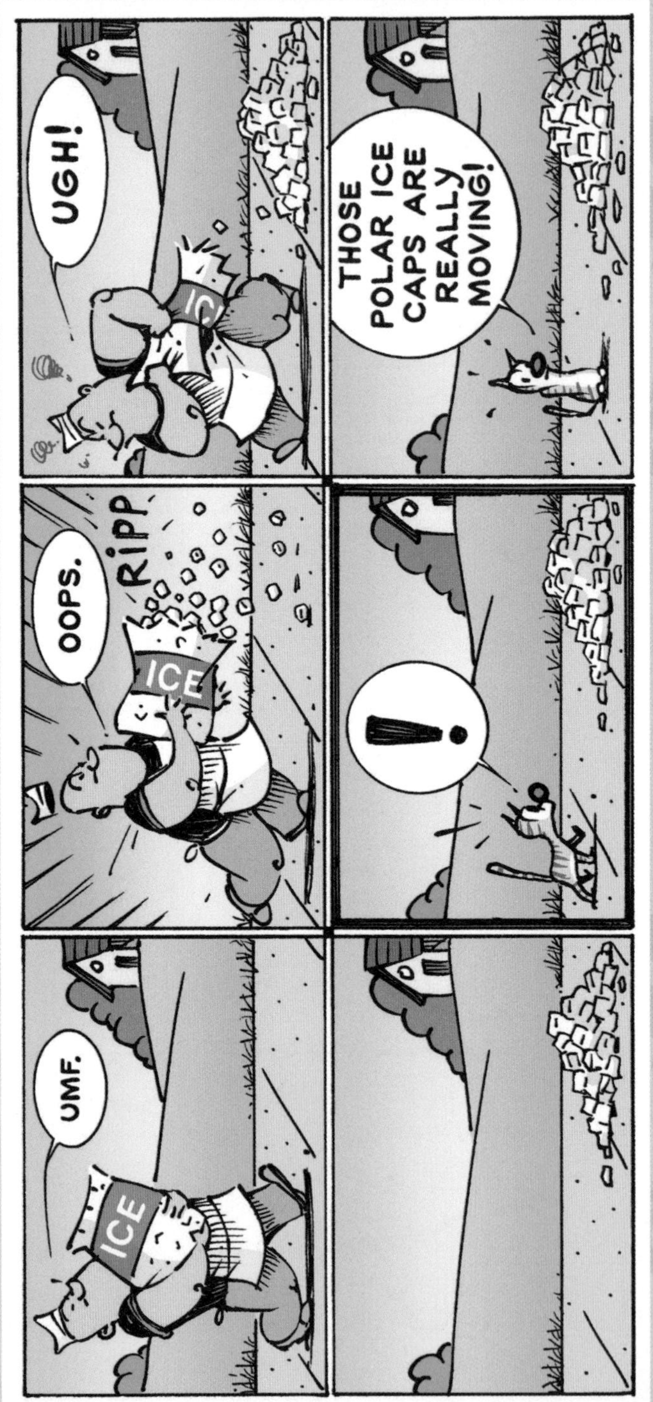
UMF.
ICE
OOPS.
ICE
RIPP
UGH!
ICE
!
THOSE POLAR ICE CAPS ARE REALLY MOVING!

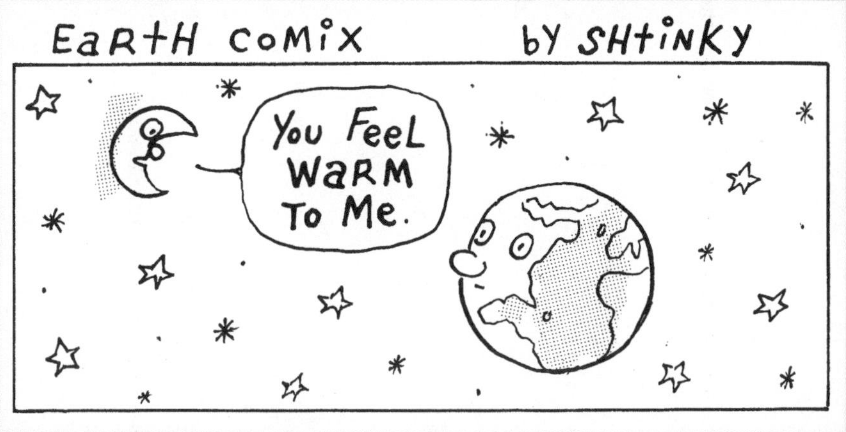
EartH coMix
by SHtinKy
You FeeL WaRM To Me.

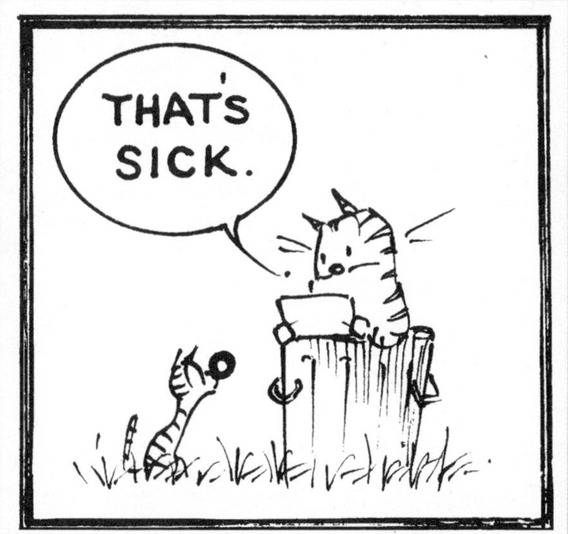
THAT'S SICK.

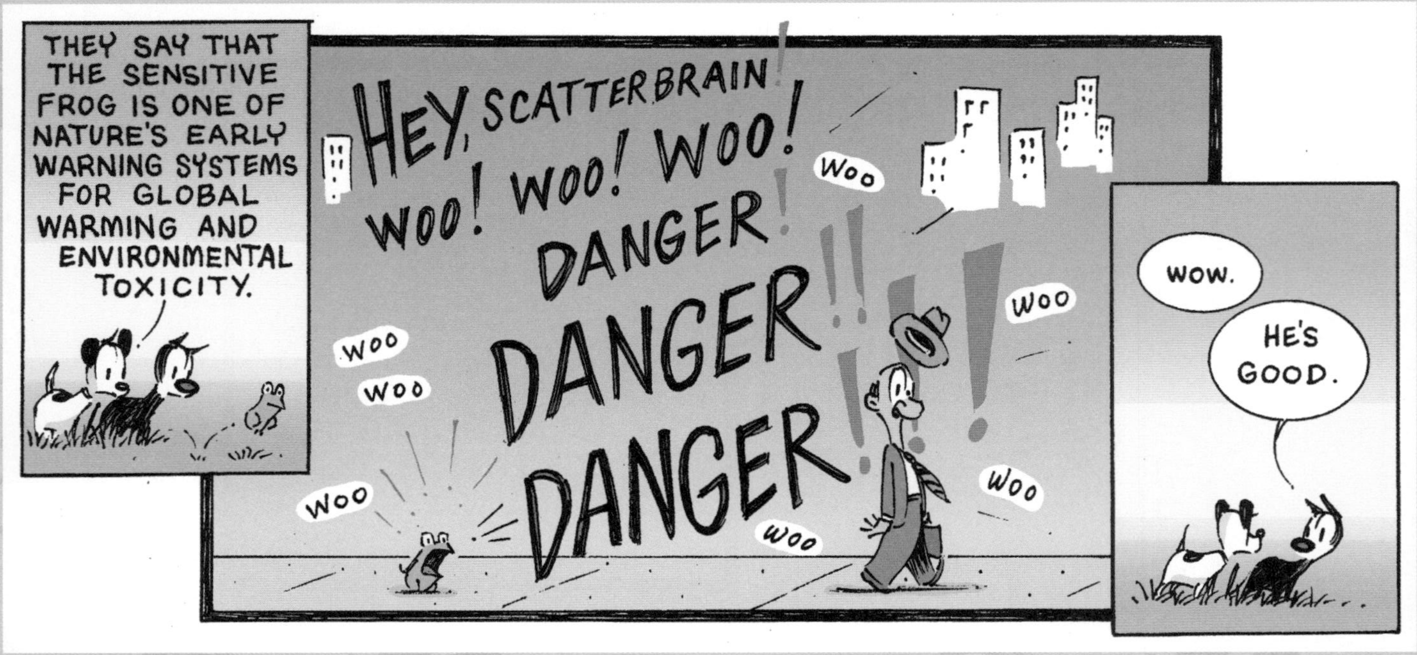
THEY SAY THAT THE SENSITIVE FROG IS ONE OF NATURE'S EARLY WARNING SYSTEMS FOR GLOBAL WARMING AND ENVIRONMENTAL TOXICITY.
HEY, SCATTERBRAIN! WOO! WOO! WOO! DANGER DANGER DANGER!!!
WOO WOO WOO WOO WOO WOO WOO
WOW.
HE'S GOOD.

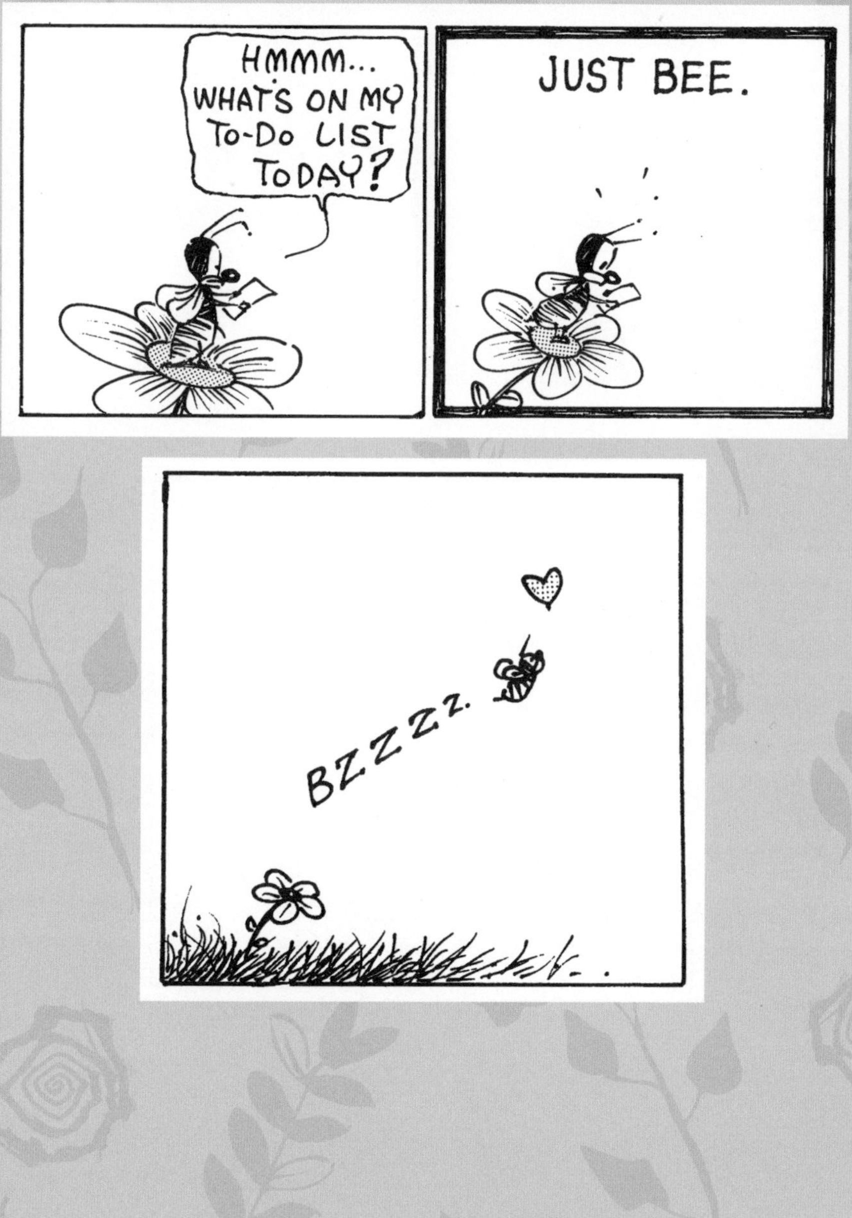
HMMM... WHAT'S ON MY TO-DO LIST TODAY?
JUST BEE.
BZZZZ.

ALLIACEOUS
A..L..L..I..A..C..E...OUS.

SHPELLING BEE.

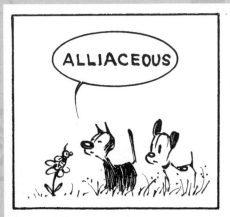

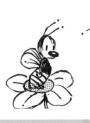

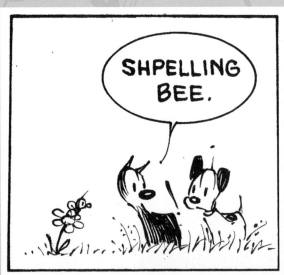

HEY, BUZZ-
WHAT'CHA
DOIN'?
MAKING
HONEY.
SHWEET.

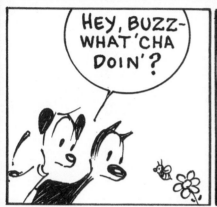

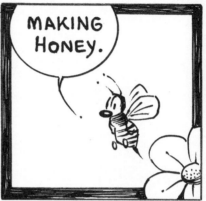

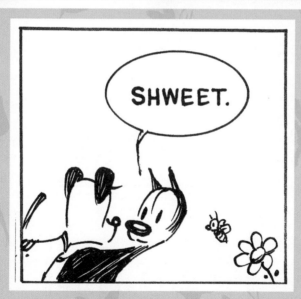

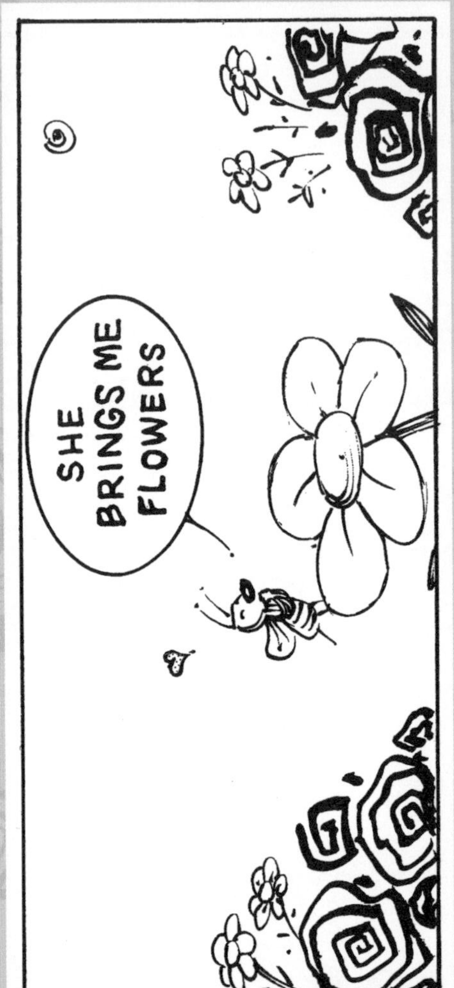
Earth Days
What do you love about Mother Nature?
SHE BRINGS ME FLOWERS

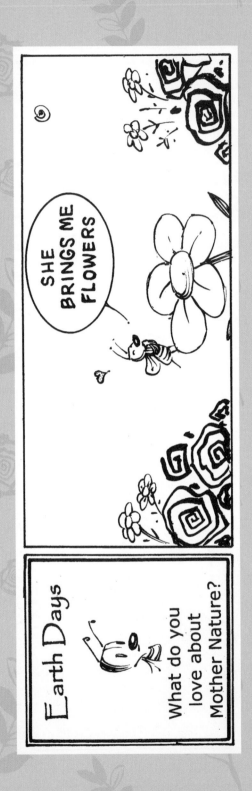

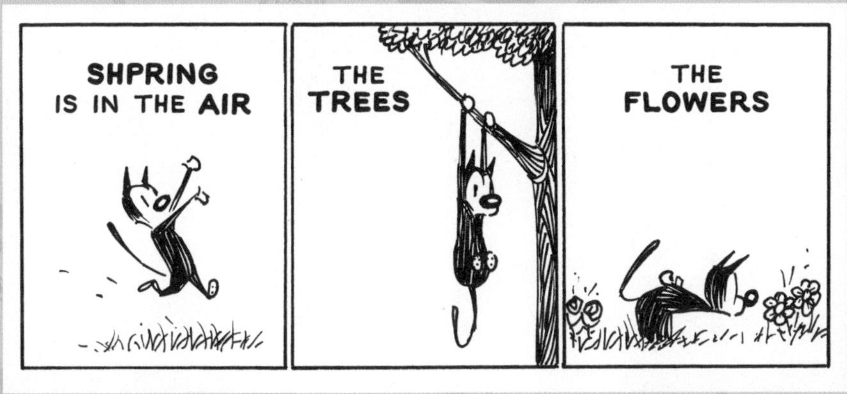
SHPRING
IS IN THE AIR
THE
TREES
THE
FLOWERS

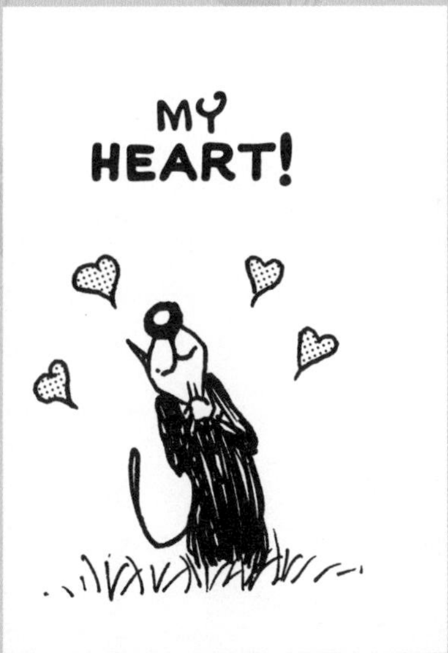
MY
HEART!

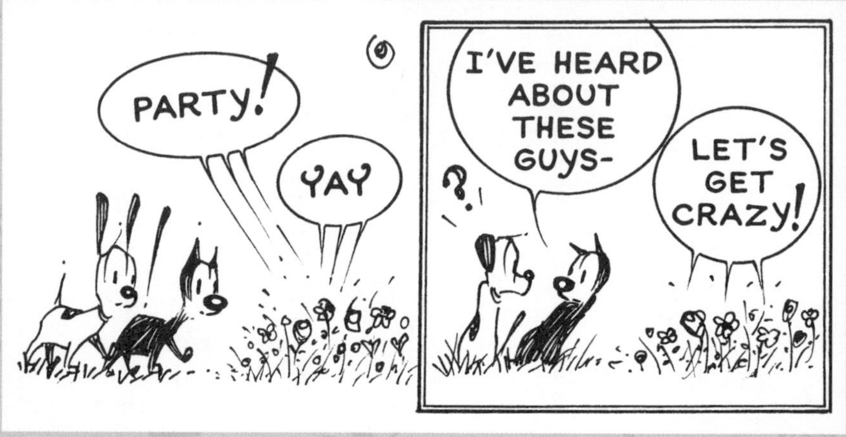
PARTY!
YAY
I'VE HEARD ABOUT THESE GUYS-
LET'S GET CRAZY!

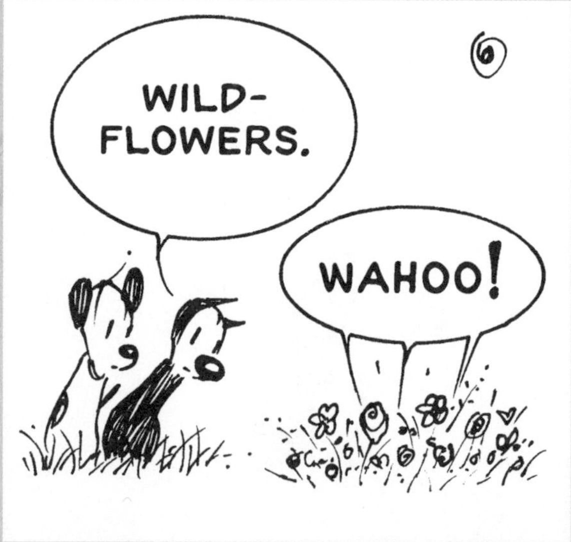
WILD-FLOWERS.
WAHOO!

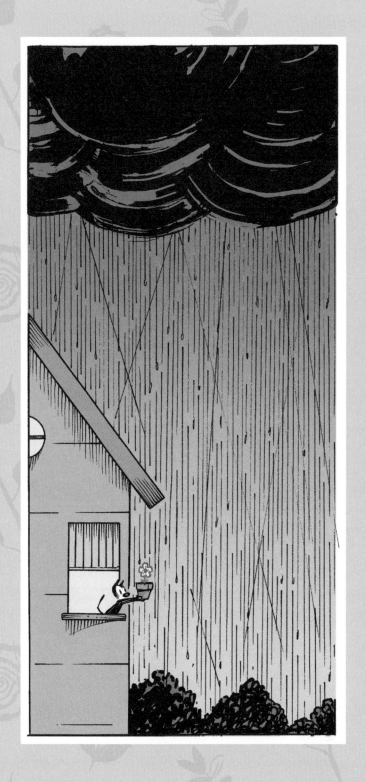

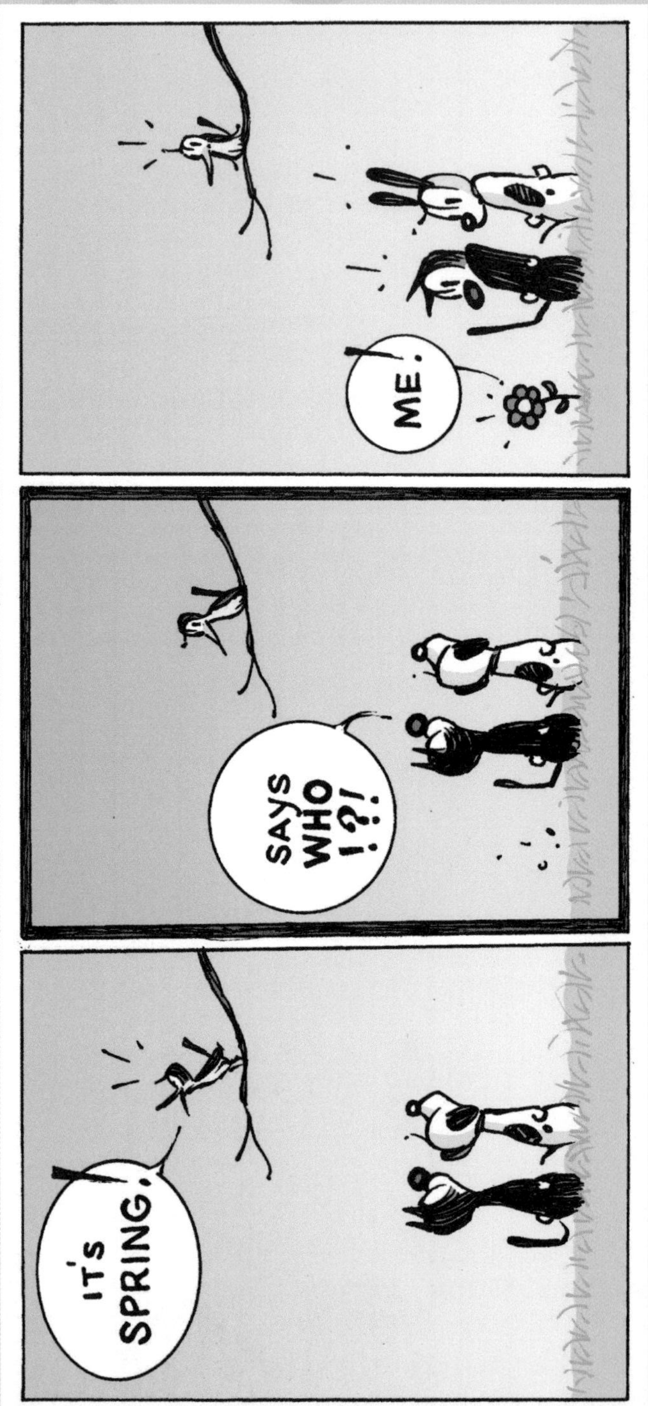
IT'S SPRING.
SAYS WHO !?!
ME.

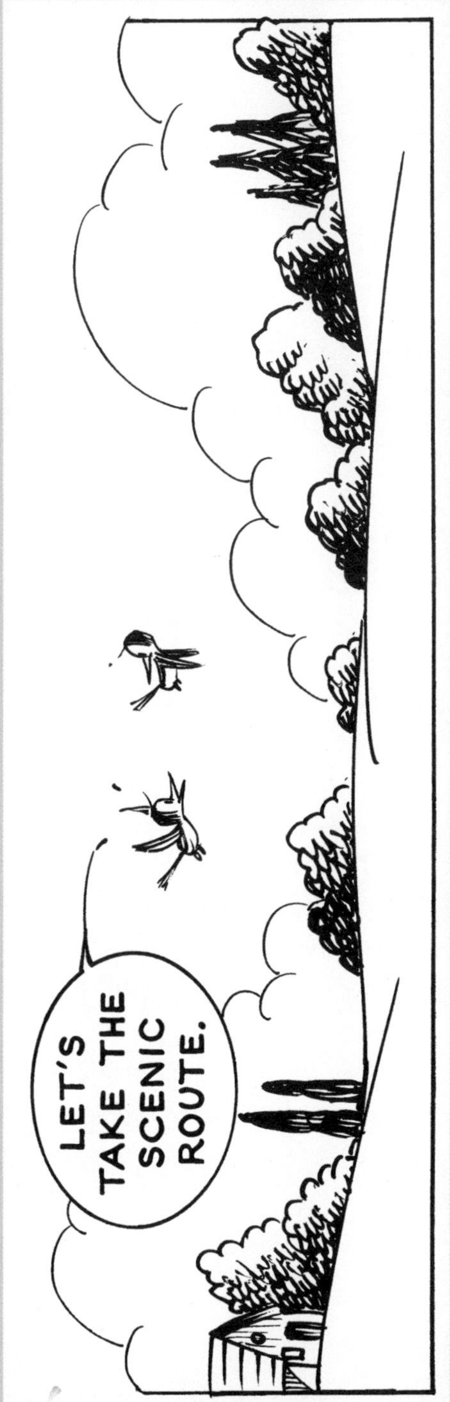
LET'S TAKE THE SCENIC ROUTE.

OOO!
HUG A TREE!
I THINK I BROKE IT.

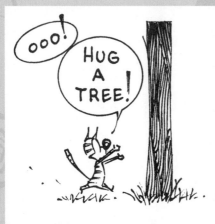

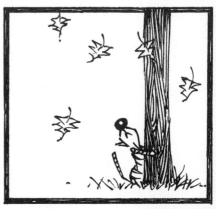

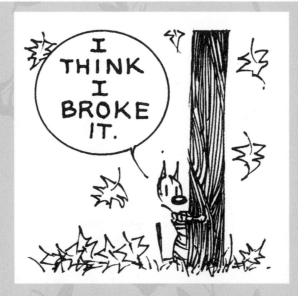

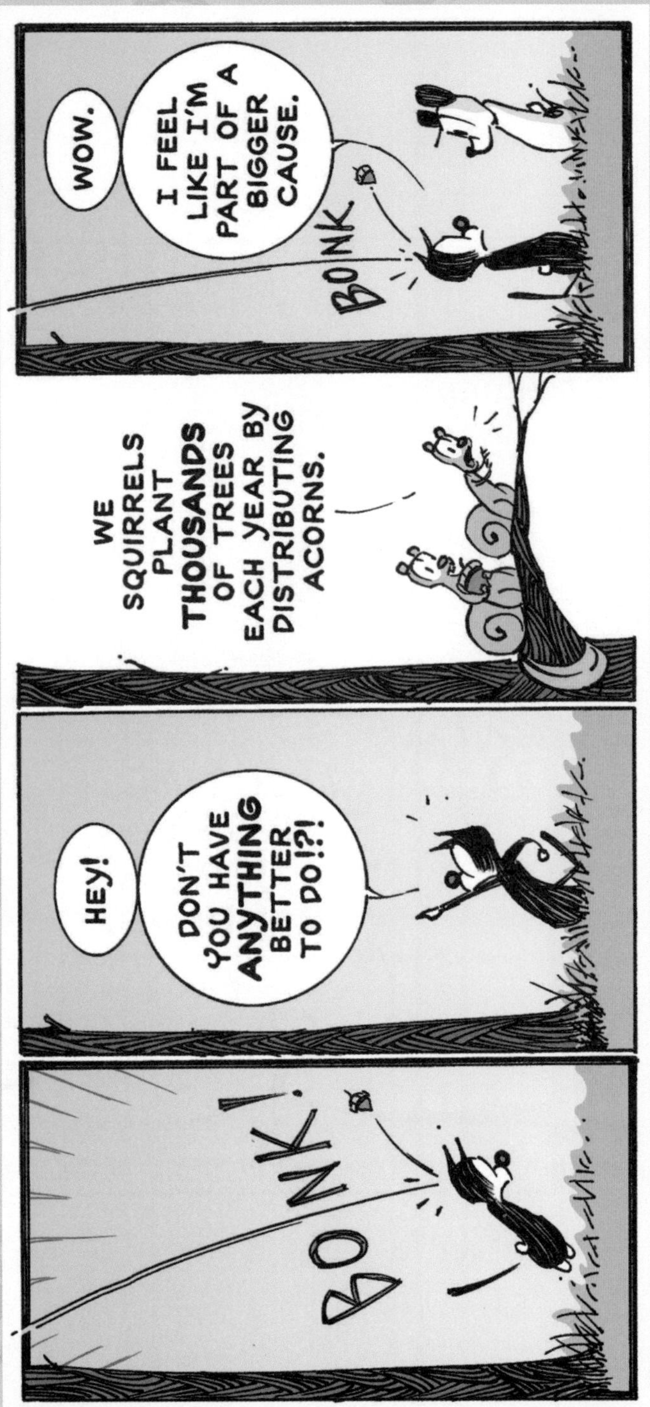
BONK!
HEY!
DON'T YOU HAVE ANYTHING BETTER TO DO!?!
WE SQUIRRELS PLANT THOUSANDS OF TREES EACH YEAR BY DISTRIBUTING ACORNS.
BONK
WOW.
I FEEL LIKE I'M PART OF A BIGGER CAUSE.

I ALMOST DIDN'T RECOGNIZE YOU...
LAST TIME I SAW YOU, YOU WERE A REDHEAD.

D'YA KNOW WHAT I LIKE BEST ABOUT CLIMBING TREES?
WHAT?
THE CHALLENGE!
I LIKE WHEN THE FIRE TRUCK COMES.

I'M ON TOP OF THE WORLD!!!
UP HERE ALL ONE'S PROBLEMS JUST FALL AWAY...

RRRRRRR

STOP! YOU CAN'T CUT DOWN THIS TREE!
OH YEH?
WHY NOT!?!
EVERY TREE IS VALUABLE! LIFE IS SO FRAGILE! OUR ENTIRE ECOSYSTEM HANGS IN A DELICATE BALANCE...

YESH.

STOP!
YOU CAN'T CUT DOWN THIS TREE!
SEZ WHO!!?!
SAYS ME!!! IT'S THE NEST-ING HOME TO THE VERY RARE LONG-TAILED LOON!!! HE'S ONE IN A MILLION!!!

I DON'T CARE ABOUT NO LONG-TAILED LOON! THIS TREE'S COMIN' DOWN!
SAVE THE TREE
SAVE THE PLANET
SAVE THE BIRD

SAVE ME DINNER !

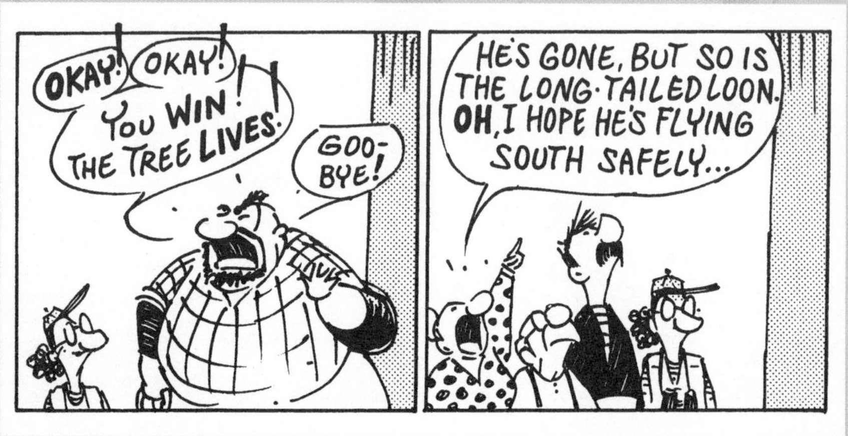
OKAY! OKAY! YOU WIN! THE TREE LIVES!
GOO-BYE!
HE'S GONE, BUT SO IS THE LONG-TAILED LOON. OH, I HOPE HE'S FLYING SOUTH SAFELY...

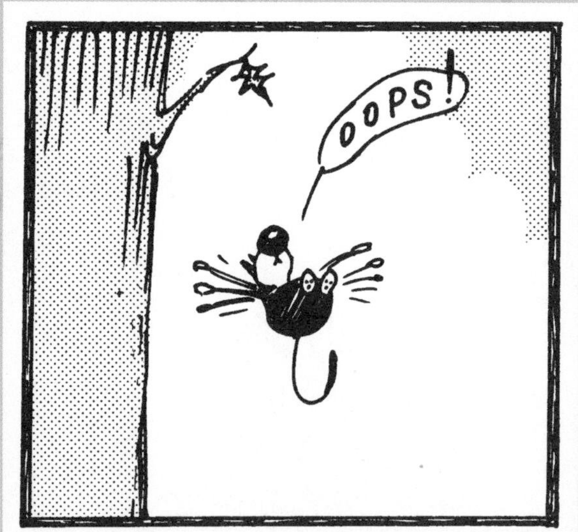
OOPS!

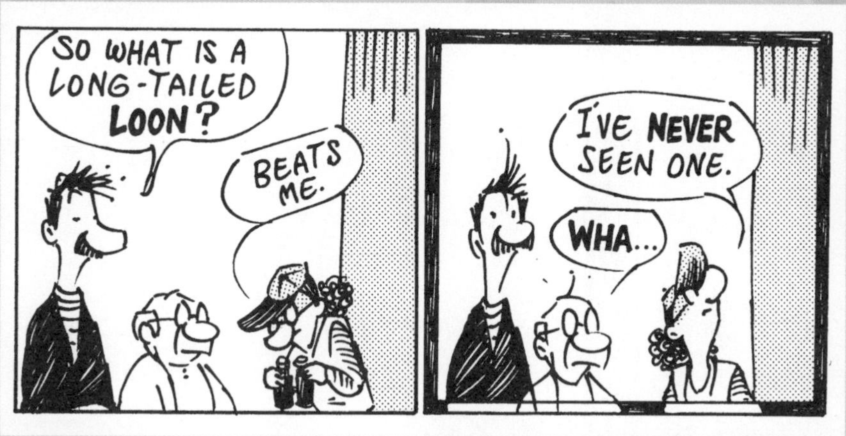
SO WHAT IS A LONG-TAILED LOON?
BEATS ME.
I'VE NEVER SEEN ONE.
WHA...

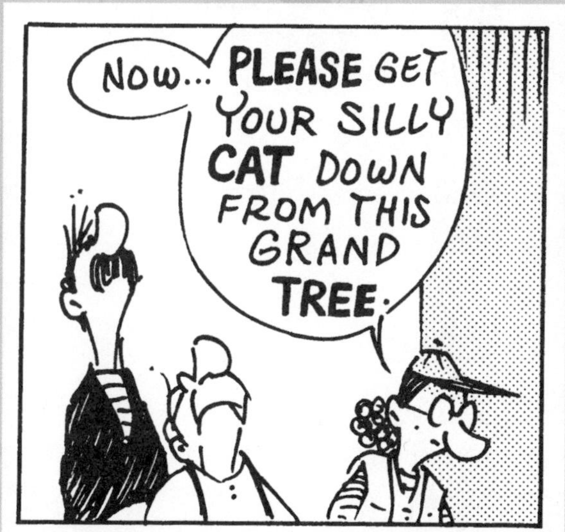
NOW... PLEASE GET YOUR SILLY CAT DOWN FROM THIS GRAND TREE.

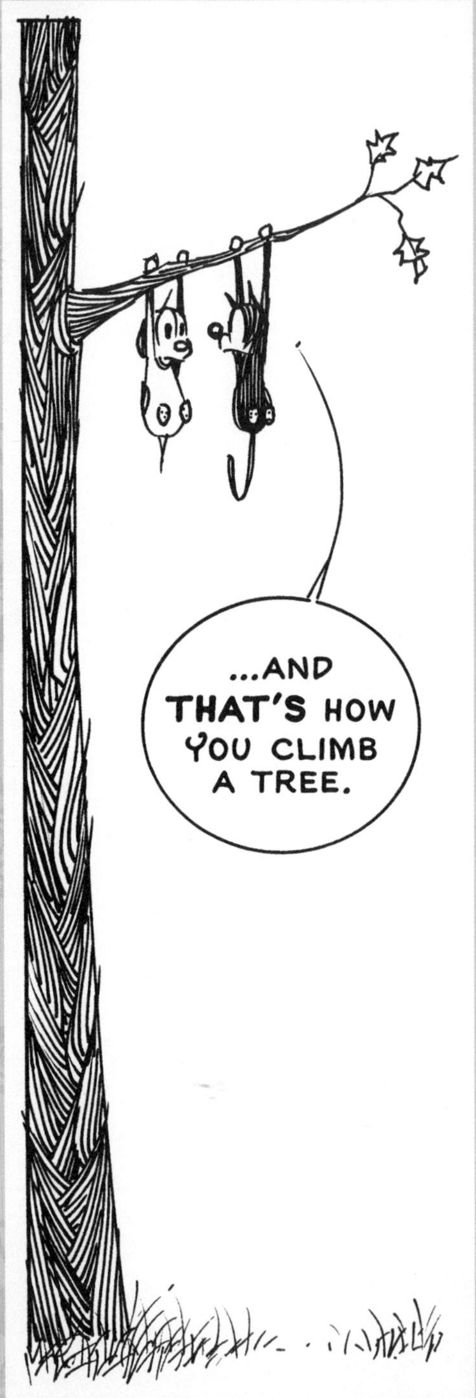
...AND THAT'S HOW YOU CLIMB A TREE.

SAY...WHERE'S OL' JOE?
GONE...
GONE!?! BUT HE WAS SO BIG AND STRONG...
...YUP... CUT DOWN IN HIS PRIME...

AHH...JOE...
...THE GOOD TIMES
WE HAD...

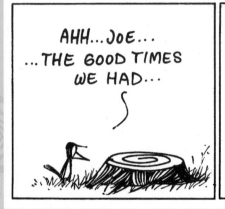

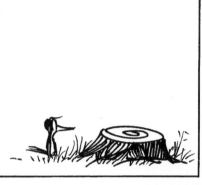

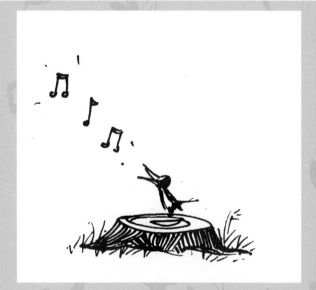

I USED TO SING IN HIS STRONG BRANCHES.
I RAISED MY KIDS IN HIS MIGHTY TRUNK.
I WOULD REST IN HIS BROAD SHADE.
HEY, I HEAR THEYRE REPLANTING TREES!
YEAH!

I NEED HELP.
I SEE YOU CAN BUILD BIG MALLS, HUGE MANSIONS, GIANT OFFICE BUILDINGS...
CAN SOMEONE PLEASE BUILD ME A FOREST?

THE NEW MALL IS "TOO BIG".
WHAT'S LEFT OF MY FOREST IS "TOO SMALL".
WHY CAN'T THEY FIND SOMETHING "JUST RIGHT"?

"HE WHO PLANTS A TREE PLANTS A HOPE."

HAPPY ARBOR DAY

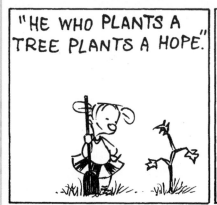

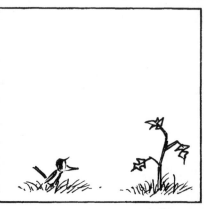

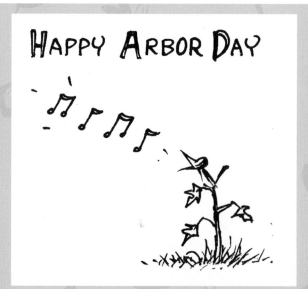

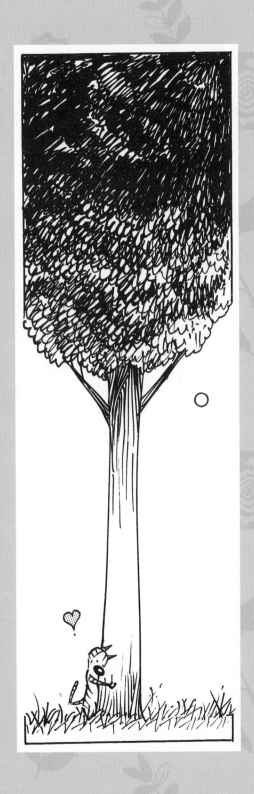

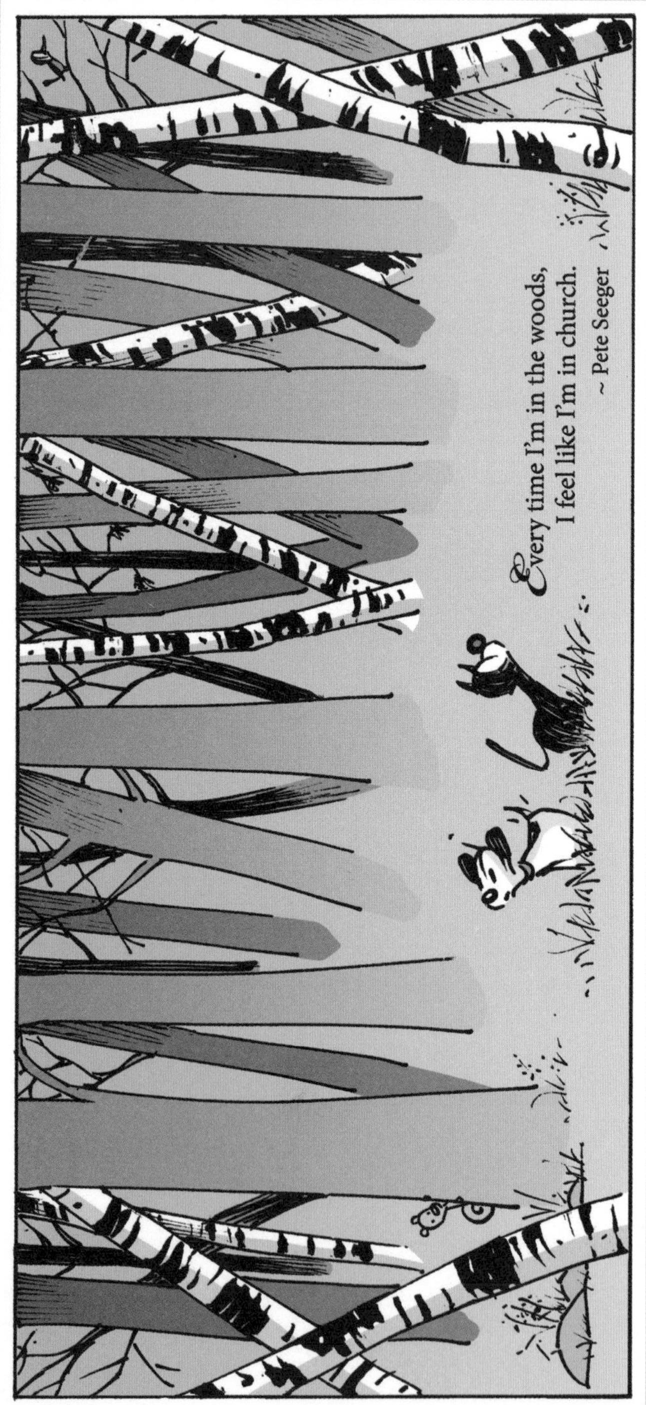
Every time I'm in the woods,
I feel like I'm in church.
~ Pete Seeger

A CHEER FOR THE HUMAN RACE.

SAVE THE PLANET YOU'RE THE MAN! IF YOU CAN'T DO IT—NOBODY CAN!

I THOUGHT WE COULD USE SOME PEP.

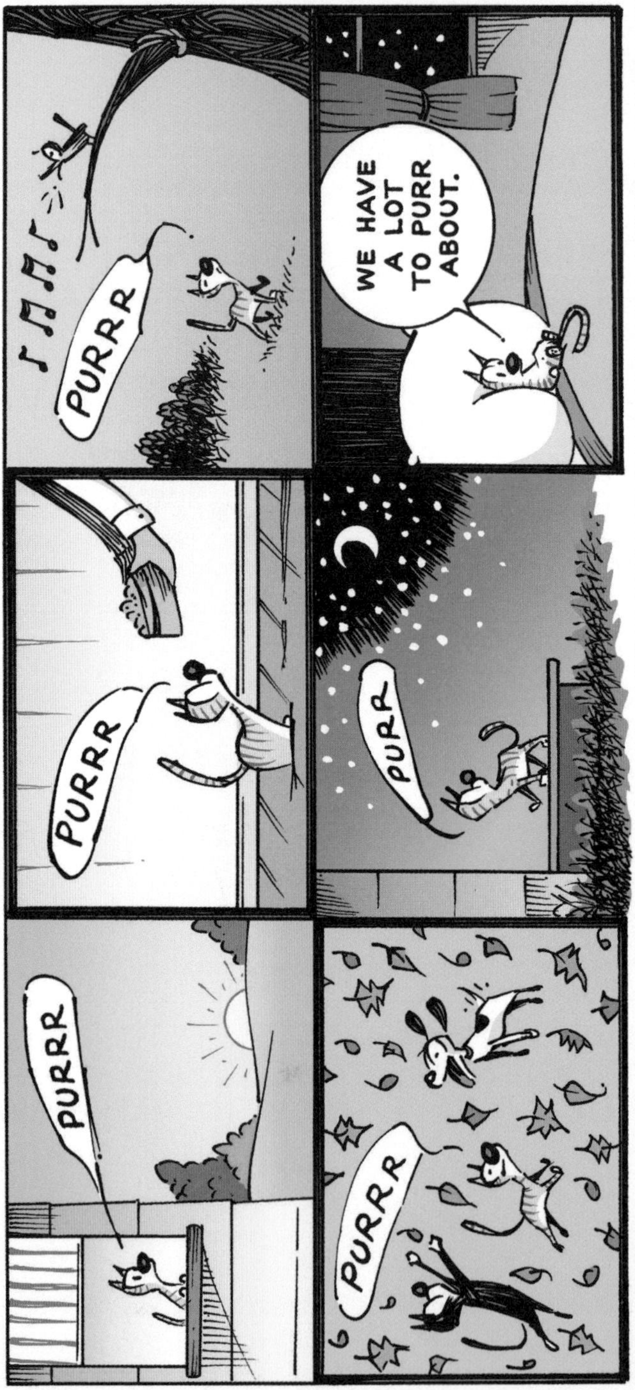
PURRR
PURRR
PURRR
PURRR
PURR
WE HAVE A LOT TO PURR ABOUT.

It's up to us to save the world for tomorrow: it's up to you and me.

Jane Goodall

Earth Days

THE MUTTS MANIFESTO

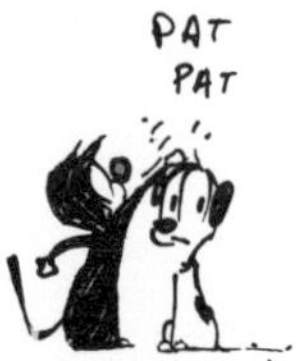
PAT
PAT

1. TO BE KIND.

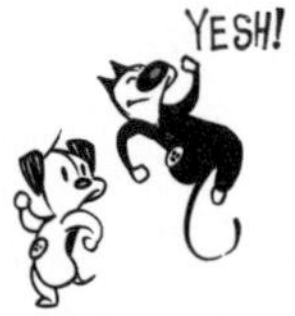
YESH!

2. TO BE PRESENT.

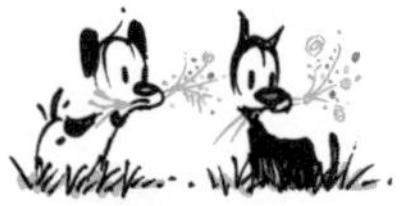

3. TO LOVE NATURE.

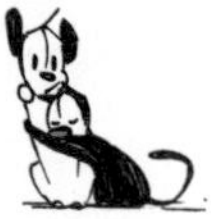

4. TO LOVE ALL ANIMALS.

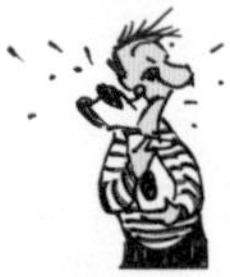

5. HUMANS TOO.

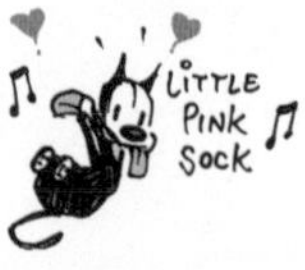
LITTLE PINK SOCK

6. TO KEEP IT SIMPLE. AND REAL.

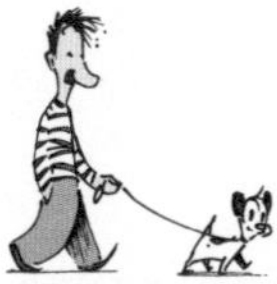

7. TO ENCOURAGE RESCUES AND ADOPTIONS.

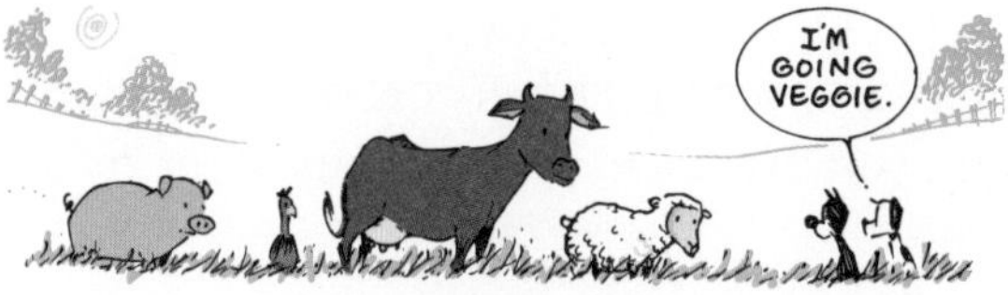
I'M GOING VEGGIE.

8. TO MAKE HUMANE CHOICES.

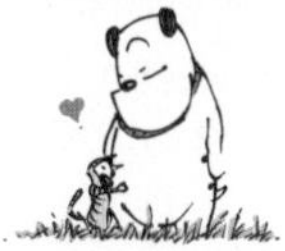

9. TO BE A POSITIVE FORCE.

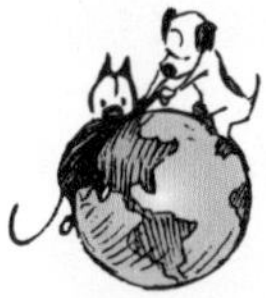

10. TO BE MINDFUL OF THE BIGGER PICTURE.

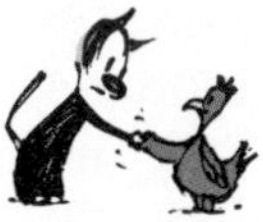

11. TO MAKE NEW FRIENDS.

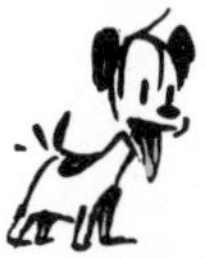

12. TO BRING SMILES TO EVERYONE EVERY DAY.

Keep It
TOGETHER

Together, we live on this beautiful planet Earth. There is so much to appreciate and so much we can do to make the world better for all living creatures. When we work together with a common purpose, there is nothing we can't accomplish. There are earth- and animal-friendly groups you can organize, as well as existing groups that you can join.

One of Patrick's favorite groups was created by one of his heroes, renowned conservationist, ethologist, and environmentalist Dr. Jane Goodall. Dr. Jane started her journey to learn and care about our planet when she was very young. Patrick created a book about her childhood called *Me . . . Jane*.

Dr. Jane has dedicated her life to saving the world. In 1960, at the age of 26, she left her home in England to travel to the Gombe forest in Africa. There, she studied chimpanzees in their natural habitat. This groundbreaking research taught us that animals think, feel, and have emotions. In 2020, Dr. Jane vowed to plant 5 million trees as part of a 1 trillion tree initiative. She is a United Nations messenger of peace and the founder of both the Jane Goodall Institute and Roots & Shoots, a program for young people. Roots & Shoots is a global movement with clubs in 60 countries. Its members have completed thousands of projects benefiting people, animals, and the environment. It gives you the tools to work together with your friends and schoolmates to build a better tomorrow. You can learn more about the movement, and how to join, at rootsandshoots.org.

Thank you for caring about our extraordinary, wonderful planet.
GO GREEN!

Mutts is distributed internationally by King Features Syndicate, Inc.
For information, visit www.KingFeatures.com.

Andrews McMeel Publishing
a division of Andrews McMeel Universal
1130 Walnut Street, Kansas City, Missouri 64106

21 22 23 24 25 SDB 10 9 8 7 6 5 4 3 2 1

ISBN: 978-1-5248-6694-5

Library of Congress Control Number: 2020945188

Printed on recycled paper.

Mutts can be found on the Internet at www.mutts.com.

Book design by Nicole Tramontana.

Made by:
King Yip (Dongguan) Printing & Packaging Factory Ltd.
Address and location of production:
Daning Administrative District, Humen Town
Dongguan Guangdong, China 523930
1st Printing — 12/28/20

ATTENTION: SCHOOLS AND BUSINESSES
Andrews McMeel books are available at quantity discounts
with bulk purchase for educational, business, or sales promotional use.
For information, please e-mail the Andrews McMeel Publishing
Special Sales Department: specialsales@amuniversal.com.

Look for these books!

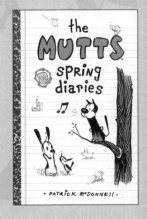

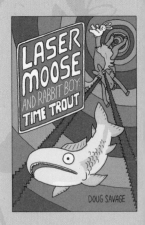